*This series wasn't planned.
It was a spontaneous project that has now become
one of my favorite story worlds.
I'd written this book after being accepted
to the Forbidden Love Book Festival.
So…thank you, Brianna.*

*And thank you to everyone
in the book community
for supporting us indie authors* ♥

The Darkota Mountain Range
Stone Mountain
Bug Canyon

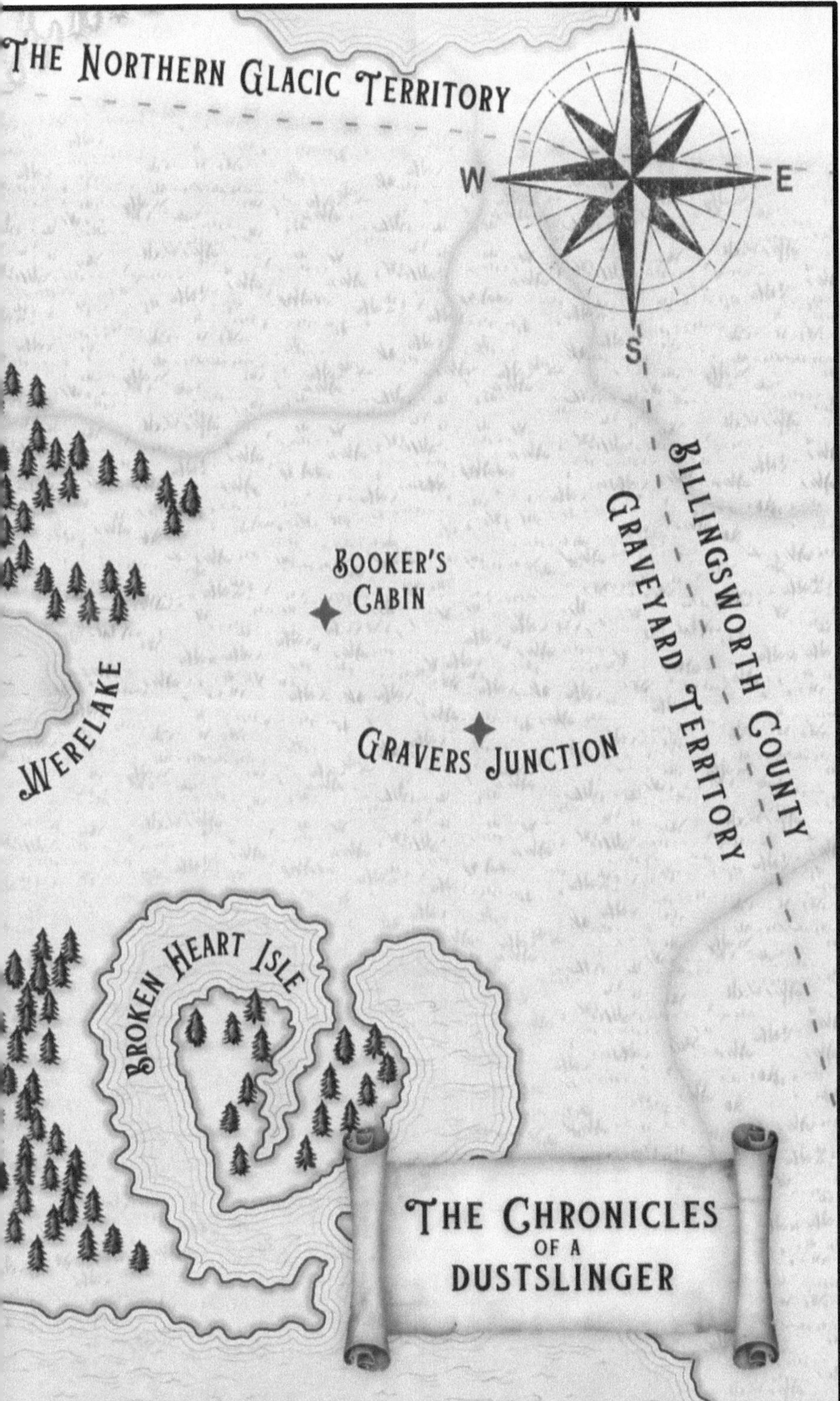

THE NORTHERN GLACIC TERRITORY
N
W
E
S
BOOKER'S CABIN
WERELAKE
GRAVERS JUNCTION
BILLINGSWORTH COUNTY
GRAVEYARD TERRITORY
BROKEN HEART ISLE
THE CHRONICLES OF A DUSTSLINGER

THE CHRONICLES OF A DUSTSLINGER
SEASON ONE ◆ BOOK ONE

SECRETS OF GRAVERS JUNCTION

KAY GRYMES

First U.S. edition

ISBN: 978-1-9652250-97 (paperback)
ISBN: 978-1-9652251-03 (eBook)
ASIN: B0GGZ9LD9T (Kindle eBook)

Cover Design and Interior Formatting by Kimberly/Kay Grymes
Character Cover Artwork by Natascia Mora (IG @moranatascia)
Book title font credit: Road Race Stamp, commercial license purchased through Creative Fabrica
Map designed by Kimberly/Kay Grymes using Inkarnate

Secrets of Gravers Junction is book one in The Chronicles of a Dustslinger series
Genre: Romantic Fantasy
Sub-Genres: Paranormal and Alternate Old West

Age Category: Adult Fiction | Not for readers 18 years or younger

Content Warning: Open door sexual content, cursing, and fight scenes

Kimberly Grymes
P.O. Box 44, Augusta, KS 67010

For more information about the author, visit https://kimberlygrymes.com/

For a deeper experience into this series, visit:
https://www.patreon.com/ChroniclesOfADustslinger

There's no cost to follow for general announcements and reveals, and you can choose to upgrade later for access to more detailed content and early chapter releases.

ONE

BEX

People say Graveyard Territory is where predators thrive and the weak die, left behind and forgotten where they fall. I'm troubled by guilt, fearing it'll be my fault if we end up lost or in a situation that's worse than death.

Hoping I'm heading in the right direction, I continue to ride east, knowing I'll have to break soon and find Tumbleweed some fresh water. She's a farm horse and not used to riding long distances. Relief washes over me when I finally lay eyes on our camp, the spot I'd left my sister at while I ventured out to explore. It's easy to get turned around in a place with no fencing and no landmarks. A wide-open plain filled with tall green prairie grass that bends in waves as a south wind sweeps over it. I don't understand how something so beautiful is feared by every man, woman, and child in our country.

Pulling on the reins and calling for Tumbleweed to slow, I reach our campsite. My sister's sitting by a small fire.

"Well, did you find anything?" Nina asks, then sips her coffee.

"Yeah," I say, dismounting. The skirt of my dress gets snagged in the saddlebag buckle, and I fumble with the fabric until I'm free. Then, before I answer, I adjust the sunrider hat on my head. The wide brim shields my face from the midday blazing sun. "I spotted a town out there. Though I'm not sure it's the right town." I lead my horse over to the small creek next to my sister's horse. They greet each other with a warm nuzzle before Tumbleweed takes a drink.

"That's not too reassuring," she says after dumping the coffee out of her tin cup. When I don't respond, she stands and kicks dirt over the glowing embers of the small campfire. "I'm guessing since you were gone most of the morning, this town you spotted is a half-day's ride?"

I finish the water from my canteen before refilling it with the cooled water Nina's boiled in the kettle. I don't have the heart to tell her I woke before the sun rose, so it's more than what she'd considered a half-day's ride.

"Hey, don't sugarcoat the distance. I can handle it," she insists. "I may be your spinster older sister, but that doesn't mean I'm an old woman who can't handle some hard riding."

This has me laughing. "Old woman, you say! You're barely a year older than me, and I feel younger than ever at twenty-seven!"

Having never found a suitor who could measure up to her high standards, because we were raised to marry for love and not wealth, Nina's accepted her marital outcome. She's lectured me on more than one occasion about how a woman can live a happy and fulfilled life in solitude. And that's when I remind her she's not alone. She's got me.

Since this isn't the time or place to be talking about her love life, I leave the matter alone. Instead, I fasten the metal cap onto my canteen and face the expansive prairie. It's beautiful. A sight I would love to wake up to every morning if I could. And honestly, I don't see what all the fuss is about, especially after exploring more of it this morning.

"Come on. Let's have it," she says, scratching her forehead while waiting on me to answer. "I know you're thinking about ways to ease my concerns, but don't. As long as we find shelter before dark, there's nothing to worry about."

It's more out of habit to sugarcoat troubled news when it comes to telling my sister stuff. She's a hard worker for sure, helping me on my small farm these past four years, but her nerves get easily overwhelmed. For as long as I can remember, after my parents took her in, Nina's had her own personal demons to deal with. Matters from her past life that she keeps private.

"Yeah, I'd say half-day's ride is about right. If we leave now, we should make it before dark. The good news is it's a straight shot from here." I point west.

"Bex, we talked about this last night," Nina warns, coming up next to me. "If we're going to sleep under the stars, we can't do it out in Graveyard Territory. You have to be absolutely sure we'll make it to town before dark."

"I know."

Exhaling a deep breath, she rests her hands on her hips. "Dammit Bex, it might not even be the right town."

"It's got to be," I say, worried the rumors of this territory have gotten to her head.

She stares at me with pleading eyes. "Why are we risking our lives to deliver some dead woman's message?"

Beneath the sleeve of my blouse, along my forearm, a faint grit stirs—more sensation than pain, like sand shifting just under the skin. I still my arm at my side, and don't look at it. Whatever's happening there, I won't give it the satisfaction of being noticed.

Her concern is justified. I've heard stories of this forsaken territory my whole life. Mothers use Graveyard Territory as an empty threat when trying to get their children to behave. And it works.

The fear drilled into the minds of everyone east of this land has kept most from venturing out into Graveyard Territory, including me. And I've never been a thrill seeker. I'm terrified for my life and my sister's. No, I do this because I have to. Looking at Nina, I silently curse, wishing she'd stayed on our farm.

Backing out of the tall grass, I move to our campsite and start packing up. "Listen, I didn't ride two days to turn back because our destination is out there. This message—it's, well, important."

Nina snorts softly and then moves to the campfire. "If it were so important, you'd tell me what that woman said. Why we're risking our lives to find her husband."

I'm not getting into an argument again about why I need to do this, mainly because the guilt of lying feels like a rock in my gut. "There's no reason for you to come with me," I tell her. "This is my errand."

She purses her mouth while shaking out the blanket she'd been sitting on next to the fire. After she's done strapping the rolled-up blanket to the back of Frostbite, she looks at me and says, "You knew the second you decided you were making this journey I'd be coming." She scoffs, brushing aside strands of blonde hair that have escaped her braids and fallen across her eyes. "You get scared and holler for me at the sight of a snake or a spider! And you expect me to believe you can handle riding out into Graveyard Territory on your own? Ha!"

"That's not true!" I snap, even though I hate snakes and spiders. "I'm a grown woman, and I can handle myself. And I'm being serious here, Nina. You don't have to come if you don't want to. You really ought to take Frostbite and head back home, or just wait here instead. I saw the town. I'll ride in, find that woman's husband, and deliver her message."

"If that's the right town," she mutters under her breath as she mounts her horse.

With my skirt held between my legs, I climb onto Tumbleweed's back. It takes a minute to get comfortable with all this bunched-up fabric, but eventually I settle into the saddle.

We walk our horses over to the edge of the dirt patch where we made camp last night and look to the prairie. Nina lifts her chin to the cloudless sky and closes her eyes. A few seconds later, the south breeze sharpens, shifting until it blows straight at us, bending the tall grass so the tops bend in our direction. My sunrider hat nearly flies off, caught only by the leather strap at my neck. Returning it to my head, I hold it in place with a gloved hand while Nina sits firmly on her horse, unfazed, as the wind picks up, blowing her pale braids off her shoulders.

Nina's life before joining our family is a mystery to me. Yet one thing she's open about is her strange connection to the winds. Well, open about it with me. Never anyone else. She says it speaks to her. I've never questioned this connection's authenticity. Just as everyone has their own spiritual practices, perhaps those from the Northern Glacic Territory, where Nina was born, worship the winds, or they believe spirits live in or manifest as winds.

After the powerful gusts fade and the grass stills, Nina opens her eyes and stares out over the vast plains. Instead of confessing what the winds conveyed, she says with a stony expression, "Last chance, Bex."

My sister is the most genuinely kind and empathetic person I know, always seeing the best in others regardless of their appearance, never judging without legitimate grounds. I envy her ability to see the world through gentle eyes. Most don't see the other side of her, the protective, battle-ready one, since we've rarely encountered threats on the farm. Her unwavering loyalty and sense of responsibility as the older sibling are things she embraces, as if they give her purpose.

"Say the word, and we turn around."

I assume whatever passed between her and the winds wasn't in our favor. "That bad, huh?"

"It's not good, that's for sure." She pulls out an old pair of leather riding gloves and adds, "It may look peaceful, but the winds tell me there's evil out there."

Tumbleweed shifts beneath me, ears flicking forward. She can sense what I'm feeling through my body and knows the difference between a pause and a retreat. I inhale a slow breath, filling my lungs. The air carries the taste of dust and sunbaked grass. Behind us lies the path home, to the farm and the house my late husband built board by board. And ahead lies a place no sensible widow would choose.

"Whatever that woman said right before she died in your arms, it can't be that important to risk our lives and ride into Graveyard Territory. There are things out there, Bex. Dangerous things, which is why no one travels it."

I don't argue. And I can't resist rubbing at my arm when the grit-like phenomenon stirs again, a persistent feeling like grains of sand moving up and down my arm. The longer I prolonged this journey after the stranger's death, the worse it got. As if whatever took root in me was alive and done waiting.

I tighten my legs and click my tongue.

Leaving the small dirt patch where we made camp last night, Tumbleweed's hooves disappear into the tall prairie grass. As if satisfied, the phenomenon stirring beneath my sleeve settles.

Nina curses under her breath and urges Frostbite to follow.

If the rumors of Graveyard Territory are true, this trip will cost me everything I have left.

I ride anyway.

TWO

BEX

We're six hours into Graveyard Territory, and I'm silently hoping we haven't veered off track. About an hour ago, we stopped at a small creek to rest the horses. Now, the sun hangs low to our left, getting dangerously close to the horizon. We're losing light faster than expected. One of my canteens is already empty, and the second is halfway there. I'm torn between pushing on and finding another creek to boil more water.

We keep at a steady trot. The prairie's openness is breathtaking. With only a few scattered cottonwood trees, there's nothing out here but wind, tall grass, and open sky above. In our favor, we've yet to cross paths with a single bandit or anything else to justify the fear folks have of this territory. This land feels like nature in its purest form, as if we're the first humans to set foot this far west.

Frostbite and my sister slow to a stop, falling behind me and Tumbleweed. "Wait, Bex. I think I see something over there." Nina straightens in her saddle and points off to her right. "Is that the town you saw?"

I follow her line of sight and spot a cluster of dark silhouettes along the horizon. "Yup. That's it."

We guide the horses, trotting through the tall grass until it breaks at the edge of town. We step out onto a dirt path that cuts straight through to the other side. I guess it could be considered a road, except it doesn't extend out like a normal road connecting communities or homes. Just a long stretch of dry dirt separating the two sides of this small town. A chill sweeps down my spine at the eeriness as there isn't a single soul walking about. I hope we didn't just stumble upon an actual ghost town.

"Look here," Nina says, gesturing to the weathered wood sign nailed to the side of the building on our right.

Welcome to Gravers Junction
Population 34

Yup. This is the place. The woman said take my message to Gravers Junction. My gaze drifts to the number thirty-four. It's carved on its own square piece of wood and fitted into the sign like a puzzle piece. "Seems like there are people here. And looks as good as any place to rest for the night," I say, hoping to ease whatever nerves Nina might be feeling. With any luck, we'll find a place to stay and the recipient of the message I carry, then be on our way home tomorrow morning.

"We're limited in our options, so yeah, this looks as good as any," Nina retorts, her expression mirroring the anxious nerves fluttering in my stomach. "We need to be careful in handling people who live this far from society. It's all about survival out here. You got your pistol ready, right?"

During our last trip into town for supplies, the general store owner sold us a rusty old pistol. It wasn't my idea, as I hate any kind of firearm. But Nina insisted we get one.

I pat the saddlebag to reassure her. "Yeah. It's in here. And don't try talking me into getting it out. I might accidentally shoot myself, or you!"

She rolls her eyes. "I should've taught you how to shoot before riding out here."

She isn't wrong, but I'm not about to admit that. I probably would've argued and whined like a spoiled child if she tried to put a firearm in my hands. Nina's always been the one to handle my late husband's old rifle whenever we hear noises outside at night or need to chase off unwelcome pests or birds. She's got that same rifle tucked in a scabbard, affixed to the right side of her saddle.

I'm about to nudge Tumbleweed forward when a dog barks from somewhere nearby. I search the road and between the buildings, but I can't spot the bugger.

"Something isn't right with this place." Nina presses her lips together, studying the worn buildings and empty road. After a long moment, she asks, "Bex, are you sure this is the place?"

I read the sign again. *Welcome to Gravers Junction.* "Yup. This is it."

With a gentle nudge of my boots against Tumbleweed's

belly, she walks the road into town. I hope the thirty-four souls mentioned on the town's sign aren't the dangerous kind. Better to be safe than sorry, I reach into my saddlebag and make sure the pistol is ready if needed. I may not like violence, but that doesn't mean I won't fight back if attacked.

Nina and Frostbite fall in beside us as we pass the first set of buildings. There are four buildings on the right. The last one is a rather large and extremely long barn-shaped structure, and it's distinguished by having two sets of wide double barn doors that open along its front side. Then to our left, there are five single-story structures, with a taller three-story building set at a slight angle and facing toward us. It's the only structure with signs of life, with soft glows of flickering candlelight in its windows.

Nina seems to notice the candlelight too. "Well, I guess we start there," she mutters.

"Mm-humph." We continue forward toward the three-story building. No one comes out to greet us or ask about our business. "Stay alert," I warn her, scanning the doors and windows.

"You stay alert," she repeats with a severe tone. "You're the one who startles easily and panics, acting before thinking and all."

A few steps along and Nina's horse falls behind. A sudden gust of wind slams into me, nearly whipping off my hat. This time I catch it before the ties pull at my neck. Looking over my shoulder, I yell, "Give me a heads-up, will ya!" But Nina has gone quiet, her eyes shut as she tilts her face to the early evening sky. She's caught in one of her trances, probably trying to find out if there's danger here.

When the wind dies and she finally looks at me, she says, "This place isn't like other towns. There's something powerful here."

"Are we in any danger?" I ask, holding Tumbleweed still as Nina guides Frostbite up to us.

"I don't think so. But there's something different about this land." She studies the dirt road beneath our horses. "A powerful energy coming from beneath the ground."

"Is this the feeling you mentioned last night? How you felt something calling you?"

"Maybe." She falls silent again as we proceed forward, accompanied by the steady *thud* of hooves and the *clink* of metal buckles and chains. After a long moment, she says, "Actually, I don't think it was this place or whatever energy's coming from the ground that called to me. The feeling here is different than what I felt by the campfire last night. Whatever's here is incredibly powerful. It's like the tornado version of what I can call when speaking to the winds. I don't know how else to explain it."

I reach over and place a hand on her forearm. "Hey, it's okay. That's not why we're here. Whatever you're feeling, we'll be on our way by tomorrow. Leaving this place behind us."

She nods in understanding. She looks over the town again, and I notice her favorite dress, the cream-colored one with little blue flowers on it, is in need of a good wash. I glance down at the skirt of my dress and think we both could use a hot meal and some clean clothes.

"How about we go and try to find a place to hole up for the night?"

"That sounds good." She smiles. "We both need a good night's sleep." As we near the tall building, she adds, "We do what we came for, get some rest and restock what we can, and then head out at first light."

"Agreed," I say, looking down at my dress. What I wouldn't give to soak in the one luxury my late husband splurged on when building our farmhouse—our copper tub. Levi took his time building our home, slowly over time and by hand. Eventually, he'd saved up enough money from working at his family's ranch and bought that damn tub for me. At first, I'd hated it, knowing we could've invested his earnings in a more practical way. Over time, I grew to appreciate it. Now, after three days of riding, my whole body aches for a hot bath.

Both horses come to a stop when the dog barks again, sharp and alarming. Both Nina and I search out where the dog's hiding. Amidst my search, I note the weathered sign above the double doors to the three-story building. The words are faded, but it reads: *Gravers Inn*.

An inn. Oh, thank the gods.

"Over there," Nina calls, and points to the shaded area between the inn and the last single-story building lining the left side of town. The inn sits at an angle so its front faces the road into town. A stout oak tree grows in the tapering space between the two buildings, its branches casting a heavy shadow that stretches toward the dirt street. Inside that darkness, I finally spot the mutt. A medium-sized, scruffy black dog stands, watching us. While it isn't growling, its tail is also still, so I reckon we keep a good distance.

I click my tongue and guide Tumbleweed forward until she reaches the hitching post beside the trough. Nina and I dismount and take a moment to straighten the skirts of our dresses, which've twisted during the long ride, before securing the horses.

"I see a pump over there." Nina grabs a metal bucket from beside the empty trough. I follow and grab a second bucket sitting by the pump. Together we fill them, the cold water splashing onto our boots, then carry them back to the trough.

"You two lost?" A man's voice behind us makes me jump. My fingers slip and the bucket tips. Water splashes down the front of my dress.

We spin toward the porch of the inn where a tall man stands, pale skin flushed as if he has been working under a harsh sun. Light brown hair pokes from beneath a wide leather sunrider hat and trails down into a short beard along his jaw.

Guilt settles in my chest as I take in the man's height and solid build, and before I can stop myself, my thoughts drift to Levi. To what he looked like. My late husband was a good man. Not the most handsome nor the sort women whispered about, yet he possessed a kind, stable, and loving nature.

That should have been enough. It *was* enough.

So why does this feel wrong? Why am I measuring anyone against him at all?

I lift my gaze again, only to find the man's eyes briefly on me before they return to my sister. My fingers curl into the fabric at my side, and I look down, suddenly aware of the dirt smeared across my skirt and the damp water stain darkening the fabric. A tight knot of embarrassment coils in my gut—until that strange sensation ripples along my skin again, drawing my attention back to him as he speaks with Nina.

Nina pours the last of her water into the trough and answers him. "No, sir. We're not lost. We're right where we ought to be."

I empty my bucket, step aside, and let Tumbleweed and Frostbite drink. Facing the man again, I see he's stepped off the porch, the raised wooden platform that stretches along the row of buildings. It forms a continuous walkway through the town, linking each storefront.

"What business do you have in Gravers Junction?" he asks, pushing his hat back, revealing more of his face. The late sun catches the brim as he folds his arms across his chest. His gaze settles on Nina. Of course it does. Her sharp cheekbones, icy blue eyes, and pale hair are so unlike the majority of folks born and raised in Billingsworth County with brown hair and eyes, and simple faces. The local men in town are always drawn to my older sister. She's just never drawn to any of them.

A crawling sensation prickles to life and the roughness of sand stirs like bracelets turning around my wrists. My heartbeat thuds against my ribs.

"Nina," I whisper. I don't know why the phenomenon that afflicts me reacts to him, but I don't like it.

She draws herself up straight. "We're looking for a man."

The corner of his mouth lifts. "And what do you plan on doing to this man? I may be of service, depending on what you have in mind." His smile widens, and he winks.

The nerve of this man. I'm torn between slapping him for speaking so boldly to two women and the unexpected curiosity to learn more about him.

The gritty phenomenon continues to caress my wrists, and I realize it's a quiet reassurance that he's not dangerous. For a split second, I appreciate its presence, but then I remind myself that whatever that woman inflicted on me is unnatural, and I want it gone.

I dip my chin and lean forward, my voice hushed, and with a sharp tone I tell him, "Sir, you are mistaken. We are not that kind of women."

He laughs even louder. Arms still crossed, he shakes his head. "No, I figured you weren't the working type."

"I'll have you know we are hard workers. We manage a farm—" Nina clarifies, but I grab her shoulder and turn her away and whisper, "That's not the kind of *work* he means."

"What?" she asks with apparent confusion, then catches my wide-eyed glare and my pointed finger directed at the area between her legs. Her face shifts in shock as comprehension clicks into place. She gasps and abruptly faces him. Wriggling her hands out of her riding gloves, she fumes over each word as she says, "I should come over there and slap you."

His brows rise, and his smile widens. "Lady, if you slap me, I won't hesitate to return the gesture. And mark my words, you'll enjoy my kind of slapping."

Both of us gasp. My voice jumps out sharper than I intend. "I demand you withhold your inappropriate thoughts right now."

"You demand, huh?" His brows hike and he shakes his head, then with a more serious tone, he reiterates his initial question. "Tell me again. What business do you have here?"

"As I was saying," Nina continues, taking a small step closer, "we're looking for a man who may have lost a wife. Are you missing one of your local women?"

Cocking his head, he shifts his weight to the other foot before answering. "All our married women are here and accounted for. You must be mistaken."

"No," Nina insists. "The woman said he'd be here."

"And I'm telling you there's no man in this town missing his woman." Any pleasantries he had moments ago are fading fast.

Nina looks to me, and she's just as unsettled as he is. "Tell him, Bex. Tell him about the woman and her message."

I tip my sunrider hat off my head, letting the leather straps catch at my neck. I try to swallow, but my throat has gone dry.

"Bex, go on," Nina says, her tone sharpening with impatience.

The man looks a little older than Nina, perhaps a year or two. Then again, looks lie. His eyes are steady and kind—more concerned than anything. No hint of malice. Strangely, the sand continues to ease my thoughts about him being a threat, even though he was insulting us with inappropriate behavior not moments ago.

Fine, I think to the mysterious phenomenon that has become my skin. *I'll give him the benefit of the doubt. Now, please be still.* The sensation of its existences comes and goes, and when it's not stirring, my skin feels normal.

Dammit. Enough beating around the bush. I need to relay this message and find a damn remedy so we can get back to our normal lives.

"Who are you really here to see?" he asks, focusing his gaze on me.

For now, we have to trust this man. Lifting my chin, ready to face whatever happens next, I say, "I need to speak with Maureen O'Callaghan."

The moment I say her name, his curious expression shifts to a hard, defensive one. As though I spoke something forbidden. He slowly uncrosses his arms, and I watch as his right hand drops to his firearm, holstered at his belt. He doesn't draw it, but his hand suggests he's prepared to use it if needed.

His dark glare remains locked onto me. "You're here for Mrs. O'Callaghan?"

"Who is Maureen O'Callaghan?" Nina's whisper is barely audible and carries an edge, as if she's just uncovered a deception. I can't blame her. I kept the real recipient from her, but what's done is done. And I need to speak with Maureen.

"I thought we were here to see a man—the woman's husband?" Nina moves so she's standing in front of me, but I step around her.

"Is she here?" I hold the man's glare.

His right hand flexes, fingers wrapping around the handle of his pistol. "I see what's going on here," he finally says, shuffling closer. His boots kick up dry dirt with each step. "You'd best tell me real fast who sent you and why. Otherwise, things are going to get real ugly for you two."

A glint of light catches my attention, and I look up to the roof of the building next to the inn. There's a man with a rifle aimed at us. Nina rapidly taps my shoulder and points over to where the mutt was barking earlier. There's another shooter, this one a redheaded woman, and she's holding two pistols, pointed in our direction.

"Whoa," I say. "You can't go around just shooting people!"

"Who sent you?" He says each word with a deliberate and final tone. His gaze darts between me and Nina while he waits to see who will crack. He steps closer, and we both shuffle in the dirt, keeping a respectful distance from him. Though the distance between us means nothing to a bullet. "Was it Cletus?" he shouts, then rambles off more names. "Or Helena…or Ambrose? Or—or… Please tell me you weren't sent by Henrik or Santana." His hand moves from his gun up to the front of his vest.

"Are they death drinkers?" the redheaded woman shouts from the corner of the inn. "Garrett! What are we doing?"

I stare into Garrett's narrowed eyes and try to understand why he thinks we're the threat. He reaches into the front of his vest and withdraws what appears to be a whittled stake.

"I won't ask again. Which Graveyard outfit do you work for?"

Too many names. Too many assumptions. And now he thinks we're working with outlaws? How dare he! I nearly march up to slap the foolishness out of him, but something tells me he wouldn't take it playfully this time. He seems perfectly serious about ending us in the middle of this dusty nowhere town.

"Garrett. That's what they called you, right?" When he nods, Nina gestures to her dress and then mine before continuing to say, "Do we look like we're working for an outlaw gang?"

"Oh, I ain't falling for that again. Santana's a sneaky bastard. Wouldn't put it past him to send a couple of fine ladies to slit our throats and drink us dry while we sleep!"

"How dare you!" I can't hold my tongue any longer. "I don't know what kind of women you're used to out here in Graveyard Territory, but we are *not* from here, and we surely don't intend to"—I lower my voice, as if the words themselves might shame me—"maim anyone in their sleep. And we certainly didn't ride all the way out here to drink your bar dry!"

"Drink our bar dry…" he echoes, brows pinching and nose wrinkling up as if he's just got a whiff of something foul. "What in all the hells are you talking about?"

Nina lifts her hands in a peaceful gesture. "Listen, mister, I think there's been a misunderstanding. We don't know who or what you're talking about. We're from western Billingsworth County and we've been riding three days to deliver a message I thought was meant for some woman's husband"—she fixes a hard stare at me—"but apparently, we're here to speak with a Miss Maureen O'Callaghan. If you'd kindly take us to her, and maybe offer a proper guest room for the night, we'll head home in the morning."

His posture eases, though he keeps the whittled stake clutched tight.

"You're not from Graveyard?"

"No," Nina states, her shoulders slumping and her face conveying a desperate plea. "A woman showed up on our farm, bleeding badly, and before she died, she gave my sister here a message meant for—"

"Maureen. Right. I heard ya." Garrett nods once. "She ain't gonna like it, but I'll take you to her." He turns, then pauses and faces us again. "If you're trying to pull the wool over my eyes, I swear I'll run ya through myself. Don't matter how pretty you two are." Then to the man on the roof with the rifle and the woman behind us with two pistols he shouts, "Stay on guard. I'm taking them inside the inn to talk with Maureen."

The mysterious sand along my arms momentarily stirs gently against the fabric of my dress. I'm still trying to understand what its movements mean, but right now it seems calm, content with the outcome. I choose to believe that means we're safe for the moment.

After I deliver the message, I hope this Maureen woman can grant me a cure, ridding me of this unnatural condition, so I can then return to my normal, boring, and safe farm life.

THREE

BEX

We step onto the wooden platform and follow Garrett toward the front double doors of the inn. There's a welcoming glow of candlelight in each of the front windows, though we'll see if Maureen's welcome is any better than the one we received outside. He opens the door and stands halfway inside, leaving us to wait. I look to the windows, but the glass panes are fogged with grime in the corners and along the length of the wood muntins, making it hard to see inside. A faint piano tune drifts out, a solemn melody I recognize but can't quite place. The moment Garrett steps aside and lets us enter, the music stops. The pianist's attention shifts from his keys to the strangers entering the parlor.

Positioned against the right wall that runs alongside the staircase, the piano is perfectly situated between a set of sconces. Looking around, I note several more sconces circling the room, each with a candle encased inside a milky hurricane holder. Together, they provide ample light. Four round tables near the front, a full bar in the back. I'm impressed with how clean and polished everything looks. The outside appearance of the faded siding and the weathered porch boards doesn't accurately reflect what's within, and I'm unsure whether this is intentional or if there's another underlying cause.

Jugs, jars, and bottles line the bar shelves, but I can't be sure what kind of liquor or ale is in them. In addition, a feature I have never encountered in any establishment is a tall cabinet set inside the wall between the bar shelves, which is secured by a sizable padlock. I wonder what they've got locked away in such an enormous cabinet.

The front door slams shut with a jarring *bang*. I turn to ask Garrett why he's slamming doors, but he's gone. I don't miss the iron slide-bolts along the top, center, and bottom of the double doors. They're all unlocked.

"Sheamus." A woman stands up from behind the bar counter, calling out to the pianist. "Play song number six."

The pianist nods in acknowledgment and then resumes playing, choosing a faster, lighter tune this time. It takes me a second, but I soon recognize it as one of my late husband's favorites: Buffalo Stampede.

The woman lifts a hinged section of the bar top and steps through, leaving the counter raised. Her hair, dark brown with streaks of gray, sits loose, the ends almost reaching her waistline.

"What brings you all the way out to the middle of nowhere?" she asks, her voice holding a wise, mature tone. She leans against the bar, her hands tucked behind her back. Unlike most women, she's donned a pair of men's pants. Her blouse is also altered, not having the typical high-collar style women wear. The loose fit feels more like something a working man on a farm or herding sheep would wear. The top two buttons are undone, revealing her collarbones. Scandalous. There's also a firearm hanging from her belt at her waist, which doesn't surprise me as much as the pants and altered top.

"You two aren't from these parts, are you?" she asks, probably picking up on our nervous tension.

I open my mouth to answer, but the piano tune cuts off mid-note, and silence spills through the parlor. The pianist stands so quickly his bench scrapes across the floor and almost tips over. Without a word, he rushes into the dark hallway at the rear of the room. Then, two men at a table to our left abruptly stand and follow. Their matching hair color and sharp noses make them look like father and son. They hurry after the pianist without looking at anyone except the woman still leaning against the bar counter.

This town is definitely not like other towns.

"What's happening?" Nina whispers.

"You were saying," the woman remarks as if the room didn't just clear out. She stares at us while stretching one arm out along the bar. Her fingers tap a steady rhythm against the polished wood. Her other hand remains hidden out of sight. "We aren't fond of uninvited visitors."

"What does that mean?" I ask. "We need a place to rest for the night. This is an inn, isn't it?"

"Maybe." She studies our faces, then our clothes. "Maybe we should take this outside so we don't break any furniture."

Nina loops her arm through mine and nervously squeezes my forearm. I pray she doesn't awaken the strange sand afflicting my skin. Lifting my chin, I address the woman threatening us. "Ma'am, we're not here to cause trouble. There's no reason to take anything outside."

A howl interrupts our conversation. And even though it's coming from outside, the sound stirs the sand along my arms to life. I brush away Nina's grip, not wanting her to feel the sensation of the sand that is my skin moving beneath my sleeve. Seconds later, a terrifying growl, sounding much closer than outside, sends my nerves jolting throughout my body.

"That doesn't sound like the scruffy mutt under the oak tree," Nina whispers, eyeing the room and searching for the source.

The sand beneath my skin swirls around my forearms, faster and faster. I clamp a hand over one arm, willing it to settle. *Please, please, please don't start.*

"The sun's almost set," the woman says. "If you're here to bring trouble, well, I reckon you're gonna be in the fight of your life." She nods at the front window, and I glance back. Through the grime of the glass pane, off in the distance, the sun sinks below the horizon directly over the road that cuts straight through town. "Now tell me why you are here."

I smooth my hands down the front of my skirt. "Are you Maureen O'Callaghan?"

"Aye. I am. Are you here to kill me?"

Nina opens her mouth to protest, but I squeeze her arm, silently asking her to hold back. To Maureen, I say, "A woman showed up on our farm, bleeding out, and before she died, she asked me to bring you a message."

"Is that so? A dying woman came to your farm out in…" She leaves the sentence open.

"Billingsworth County. The west side. Our farm is a two-day ride to the Graveyard Territory borders."

Maureen laughs. "You two aren't joking about not being from around these parts."

"No. We aren't," Nina says, her voice rising with frustration. "That's what we've been trying to tell you."

The beast growls louder—closer—and I glance at the window. The sun dips below the horizon, leaving a red-orange glow in its wake.

"Your time's running out, ladies," Maureen says. "I'd hate for you to meet Hunter if you're actually telling the truth."

A pair of glowing yellow eyes appears in the doorway to the hall where the pianist and those two men disappeared. It's completely dark, and the animal's predatory gaze sit at a height that makes my stomach dip. If that's a wolf, it's sure as hell the biggest one I've ever seen. And we've seen our share on the farm.

"We're telling you the truth!" Nina protests with urgency. A low growl rolls out of the shadows in response. She turns to me, her voice sharp with fear. "Tell her the message, Bex."

"All right, all right." Heat blooms under my arms as my

heart hammers at the threat in the doorway. "I don't know the woman's name, but she told me to tell you this: 'Persephone is dead. Tell her it was Malik Graves.'"

Maureen's eyes widen. She pushes off the bar, revealing a dagger clutched in her hand that had been hiding behind her back. Inhaling a deep breath, she shakes her head, causing her long brown hair streaked with gray to fall off her shoulders. "That cannot be. She was just here two weeks ago. And she would've told me if she'd planned to go off and face that miserable piece of shit." Her gaze dips to the floorboards, and she mutters a string of half-formed questions. The only one I can understand is something about "why would she go at it alone?" None of it makes sense to me.

The terror in her eyes speaks volumes, revealing the news to be more devastating than I can comprehend. Something in my chest tightens, and I shuffle closer, hating to see anyone in pain, and offer more of an explanation. "That's what she said. I don't know these names or what any of it means. But we traveled all this way to relay her message."

Nina comes up next to me, and Maureen eventually lifts her gaze from the floor to us. "Please, ma'am," Nina says, "we delivered the message. Now if you'd kindly let us rest the night, we'll be out of your hair in the morning."

The growl from the shadows deepens. Nina huddles closer and hooks her arm through mine. Her grip tightens over the fabric of my sleeve. Underneath both sleeves, the sand coils in tight, spiraling bands around my wrists and forearms, pulling inward as if preparing for something.

"There is something else," I shout over the growling.

Maureen does not speak. She waits.

"The woman, before she died…she…she did something to me." After freeing my arm from Nina's grip, I unbutton a cuff, roll the sleeve up to my elbow, and hold my arm out. My skin has loosened into grains of pale sand that drift in slow, deliberate patterns over my wrist and forearm. The sand isn't loose, but holds the shape of my arm.

"Please help me understand what this is about?" I ask. At the same time, something new sparks to life. Dust streams from the center of my palm and twists into a thin, gritty, rope-like strand, one end rooted in my hand while the rest lifts into the air. I flex my hand. The strand, made of the same sand my skin has changed to, shifts with me. It doesn't reach far, but something in my gut tells me I can extend it out… If I push it to.

Maureen steps closer, tucking her dagger into her waistband, and grabs hold of my elbow. Her fingers clasping tightly over the fabric of my sleeve. She lifts my arm to better see the phenomenon, and as she does the strange rope coming from my palm suddenly bursts into a dust cloud.

"Whoa," I say under my breath. Looking to Maureen, I ask, "What was that? What's happening to me?"

She lets go of my arm and mutters, "Well, I'll be damned. Either you're lyin' to me about what happened or we've got ourselves a new dustslinger."

"A what?"

Turning away from me, Maureen whistles and shouts, "Cage him up, boys."

The glowing eyes from the back hall retreat into the darkness.

I wait for Maureen to return her attention to me, hoping for answers, but instead she moves past us and proceeds to bolt the front doors shut. When she finishes, she gestures toward the stairs. "Come along. I'll show you two to your room."

I hurry after her, weaving between tables. "Aren't you going to tell me what's happening to me? What that woman infected me with?"

Her smile is unexpectedly warm. "It's not an illness, darling. It's a gift. A rare one. And with it comes a responsibility to fight for and protect the innocent souls of this territory. Now, before we get into the specifics"—she points to my arm—"how about we get you both settled into a nice private room. We can talk more at supper, which'll be in an hour. I'll have Garrett bring up your bags after he settles your horses in their own stalls in our barn. Don't worry, there's plenty of space and fresh hay. Now, come along. You'll want to rest a bit, maybe even take a bath, do whatever you need, and we'll speak more on the matter later." Without another word, she heads upstairs.

Did she say *take a bath*? Oh, my prayers have been answered if there's a tub up there!

Nina follows behind our host but stops on the first step and leans over the railing and points a finger at me. "You and I," she says with a severity I knew was coming, "need to have an honest conversation about all of this in private."

I swallow the guilt rising in my throat. I shouldn't have lied, and she has every right to be angry. But deep down inside, I knew I couldn't do this without her. And I was hoping I could find a remedy for this sand-skin illness without having to tell her.

Maureen saying it's a gift raises my concerns about there being a cure or a way to get rid of this supernatural phenomenon. If that's the case, what does it mean for me? Because I'm no protector. I hate firearms and wouldn't even know how to save myself, moreover an entire town of people.

I have to hope something good will come out of this trip besides delivering that woman's message to Maureen.

Following our host and my sister up the stairs, I push aside concerning thoughts about being their new dustslinger and instead cling to the promises of what's waiting for me upstairs. A relaxing, hot bath where I can momentarily escape the problems of my life.

As I reach the top step to the second floor, boots pound across the parlor floor below. Peering out from behind a post, I track the man's movements as he makes his way to the front window. It's the man we'd met outside–Garrett. He lingers for a moment, staring outside. When he turns, his gaze meets mine. Like a fool, I don't blink or look away. Slowly, a smile spreads across his face and he tips his sunrider hat. A lively pulse thrums low inside my core, and my lips part as though I've just broken the surface of a lake, gasping for air. I warn myself that nothing good will come of befriending that man, especially when we plan to return home in the morning. Nothing good at all.

FOUR

BEX

Now this is exactly what my body needs. Hot water soothes my aching muscles and quiets my anxious thoughts. I lean against the curved rim of the tub and savor the heat, my bones and muscles already aching less after three days on horseback.

Steam rises, and I breathe it in. The copper tub is much like the one Levi splurged on for our home, only longer, and wide enough that it could probably fit another person.

"Feels good, right?" Nina asks while looking at me through the mirror affixed to the wall just over the dressing table.

A small wood-burning stove heats the room, and the bucket of water is set on top, ready in case I need more hot water.

"This is nice," I admit. "There sure are a lot of modern amenities for being so isolated." Something else I first noticed after Maureen showed us to our room. My gaze drifts from my sister over to the corner of the room where a large water pump sits on a base made of the thinnest stone I've ever seen. Resting my head back against the curved rim of the tub, I stare up at the ceiling. Our room is on the third floor, and they've built a loft area up into the rafters. We don't have access to it, so who knows what's up there.

There's a beautifully crafted four-post double bed, perfect for both Nina and me to sleep in tonight. The room also has a three-drawer dresser with a ceramic washbasin and pitcher, a small bookcase full of old books, and the dressing table where Nina sits. The only thing we can't figure out is a locked door next to the main entrance.

"I'm pleasantly impressed with all the amenities in this room," Nina admits, shifting in her seat at the dressing table and holding the silver hairbrush in her lap. Her braids are unbound, letting pale blonde hair fall in waves over her shoulders. "And now that it's clear we aren't a threat, I've got a good feeling about this place. We may actually learn a thing or two about surviving out here."

"A good feeling, huh?" I ask.

She nods, brushing her hair.

"What about that strange power you felt earlier outside? The one coming from underground?"

"I don't know what that was. A fluke, most likely. My gifts aren't perfect. The winds speak to me, but I don't get those sensing feelings very often on the farm." Her gaze drifts aside. "Not like I used to, back when I was—" she stops herself. She rarely talks about her childhood in the Northern Glacic Territory, not even to me.

Sliding along the bottom of the copper tub, I rest my elbows on the edge and prop my chin on the warm metal. "What do you remember of this place back when you escaped the north? You told me once you'd been to these parts after your escape."

Her gaze drifts from me to the hairbrush in her hand. She slowly starts running it through her hair, and for a moment I think I'll get the same answer she always gives: *I don't remember exactly.*

"You probably wouldn't believe me if I told you." Her voice is low, as if she'd be okay with me not hearing her response.

But I do want to know. "Try me. What happened?"

"Bad things, judging by the screams that echoed through the night. During the day, all was quiet, an easy journey, just like it was when we were riding through it earlier today. But once the sun sets, it gets real dark out there, especially if there's little to no moonlight. You can't even see your own hands right in front of your face." Nina turns to face the mirror again, still brushing her hair, and continues "I hid most nights, barely moving a muscle, hoping whatever was out there causing all that screaming didn't find me. And then one morning, right after sunrise, I felt the pull of something. It wasn't the whispering wind, but something different. And I trusted it, and it led me to the edge of the Graveyard Territory."

"Something was watching out for you, that's for sure," I say, happy her story wasn't as bad as I thought it was going to be. Hearing those screams is bad, but thank the stars she didn't witness any of the horrors she was hearing.

She seems lost in her thoughts, and guilt rises in me for bringing up the past. Wanting to shift her mood, I say, "Hey, I'm sorry about lying to you about the message."

And that does it. The concerned look consuming her shifts to an annoyed, pinched one. "Yeah, well, you should've told me the truth. And you should've shown me what's going on with your arm."

"It's actually more than just my arm. It's everywhere. My whole damn body."

"Language!" Nina spins in her seat to face me, scolding me like when we were young. Her gaze narrows and she sets the brush down before approaching me. "Hey, what's that on your back?"

I move my shoulder so she can get a better look, unsure if maybe I scratched or bruised myself somehow.

She gasps and I take in her wide-eyed expression.

"What? What is it?" I ask, trying to look myself, but I can't see anything past the top of my shoulder.

Her finger trails over my skin, outlining something in the center of my back. "Bex, it looks like someone branded you."

"Branded me!" I almost jump up out of the tub, but before I can Nina goes over to the dressing table and pulls out a handheld mirror from the drawer. She hands it to me, and I hold it at an angle so I can see the mark she's talking about.

"What on earth is that?"

"It's a brand!" she reiterates and moves in closer. "It looks old, scarred over like you've had it for years."

I lower the mirror. "We both know I've never had a brand

or a scar on my back." Lifting it up again, I look in the reflection at the mark. It's a circle with an upside-down triangle in the middle, and the top part of the triangle is more center than across the top.

"It looks like an upside-down A, if you ask me," Nina states.

I look again, and she's right. It's not an upside-down triangle but an upside-down A. "What does it mean?"

"How am I supposed to know? You're the one with the brand!" She takes the mirror and returns it to the drawer. Then crossing her arms over her chest, she offers me an answer. "Maybe it has something to do with whatever's happening to your body. This dustslinger stuff."

I groan out a sigh and rest back against the tub.

Knock. Knock. Knock.

We both go silent and look at the door. Nina answers, only cracking the door open enough to greet whoever it is, making sure they don't have a view of me in the tub. I duck lower below the rim, just in case they can see inside the room.

A man's muffled voice floats in, and after she closes the door, I ask, "Who was that?"

"It was that handsome man who greeted us on the street earlier. Garret, I believe was his name. He said supper is about ready." She sits on the edge of the four-post bed and asks, "You wouldn't have noticed how handsome he was too, by any chance?"

"Nina, please! I know you feel it's your new purpose in life to keep me company after I lost my husband, and I'm grateful for that. Truly, I think that's all I'll ever need is you company. I have no desire to commit to a man.”

“First of all, thank you for your kind words. And second, maybe one day I’ll find the right man and settle down. Then what? You’ll be all alone on that farm of yours.”

“I doubt it!” I tease, smiling. “You set the bar so high, I don’t know who’d ever measure up.” Nina feigns a hurt expression, pressing a hand to her heart. I soften my voice. “You know I want the best for you, and I do hope you find that special someone you can love and grow old with. I’m just a little selfish in wanting you around for a bit longer.”

She works her fingers through her hair, braiding one side of her hair. “I know you loved Levi, but he’s gone. And you’re still young, just starting your adulthood. Don’t give up on finding another to love. Okay?”

I nod. It’s the best I can offer. Then I offer her another side of my reasoning, and say, “Our life isn’t here. It’s back on our farm. So, even if a certain handsome man were available, his life is here. Why would he leave this place? So, no more talking about finding love, all right? Not while we’re out here in Graveyard Territory.”

“Fine.” Then a wide smile spreads on her face as she sits on the edge of the bed. “But you admit…he is a handsome man.” After tying the end of her braid, she gets to work on the other one. “I know what he said outside earlier was inappropriate, but I have to admit, the idea of slapping in a playful manner had me curious.”

“Nina!” I’m completely taken aback by her confession, which is so unlike her usual behavior. “I’ll admit no such enjoyment. I’ve gone four years without a man, and I don’t need to depend on one now. So, if you don’t mind heading down to supper, and leaving me to my bath? I'll follow shortly."

We both chuckle. My sister and I weren't always this close as youths. It's only been during our adult years, after Levi's death, that we've grown closer, which has made Nina more comfortable talking to me about her connection to the whispering winds.

After she finishes tying her second braid, she dumps the bucket of hot water from the stovetop into the tub, reviving the steam. Then she grabs a knitted shawl before leaving me to my indulging deeds.

It doesn't take long for me to lose myself in the hot water. My hands drift slowly back and forth under the surface, forcing the water to swirl around my body. This may not be my tub, but it's easy for me to fall into a familiar routine. I let one hand sink into the water, caressing the inside of my leg, until my fingers reach a place I've tried hard to ignore. Soft moans escape as I sink lower into the tub, my mouth dipping beneath the waterline to stifle the sound. My other hand finds my breasts and caresses them one at a time, working in sync with the pleasure pulsing between my legs.

The tub has plenty of room, and I take full advantage of the space, lying back. The room fades at the edges of my vision as I stare at the ceiling, my head floating just above the water. All sound vanishes as water fills my ears. I stay here, knees bent as my hands continue caressing and rubbing, giving my body a pleasurable numbness. For the moment, I have no worries…no pains or heartaches…just internal bliss.

When satiated, I plunge my head under and stare up with my eyes open, looking at the world through the surface of my bathwater. Is this what it's like to be a spirit in the afterlife, wandering about and observing the living? To see us as if looking through an altered window?

Pressure tightens my chest, and I force myself to push through it. Can I endure pain? If what Maureen says is true, that this sand affliction is a gift and that I have a responsibility to fight and protect the innocent of this territory, I'll have to learn more than just how to handle a little pain.

The pain intensifies, but I don't surface. I can do this. The burn in my lungs sharpens, and just as I'm ready to give in, hands suddenly grip my shoulders and haul me up. I break the surface with a deep breath, sucking in air as I struggle to shove my assailant away. Water burns beneath my ribs as I cough, spitting it from my lungs.

"Get away from me!" I shout between coughs, scrubbing water from my eyes.

"Oh my gods, I'm so sorry," the man says, panic and embarrassment tangling his voice. "I thought you were drowning."

My vision clears enough for me to see it's Garrett. "Turn around!"

His blurred shape pivots instantly. "I knocked," he says quickly. "You didn't answer. I knocked again, and when you still didn't respond, I thought something was wrong. So I—"

"You decided it was acceptable to enter someone's bedroom uninvited?" I stand, crossing one arm over my breasts as I step from the tub and lunge for the towel on the bed. The jerk still manages a glance before I'm covered.

"My apologies, ma'am," he says, sincere enough to contradict his earlier playful, suggestive behavior.

Heat floods my face as embarrassment and unease collide. I want him gone. "Why are you still here?"

"Right, sorry." His boots pound against the floorboards as he rushes out of the room, practically slamming the door shut.

I follow and slide the locking bolt through two striking plates affixed to the door. Catching my breath, I find the edge of the bed and sit, not caring about the heavy quilt getting wet. My thoughts are all over the place. I'm furious that he entered my room without being invited in…I'm furious that he saw my naked body…and more than anything, I'm furious at myself for not thinking I betrayed Levi. That another man has seen parts of his wife that only he should see—but he can't anymore. He's gone. He left me alone with so much life left to live.

"Dammit!" I curse under my breath. The thoughts racing through my mind are too overwhelming, and I can't hold back the tears. I don't want to let Levi go, but this embarrassing moment makes me realize I have to stop worrying about hurting my late husband's feelings. I think it's time to stop clinging to the past and be open to life's possibilities.

FIVE

BEX

After putting on my last clean dress, I make my way down to the main-level parlor. Night has fallen, and about half the sconces in the parlor have been snuffed out, creating a peaceful ambiance. No one's around, but there are voices coming from the back hallway. That same hall where those mysterious glowing yellow eyes watched us from the darkness. Now, it's full of light, making it so I can see the short corridor beyond the doorway. As I approach the threshold, I note the two closed doors on the right side and two open doorways on the left. There's a larger door at the end of the hall. I'm guessing that door leads outside, considering it's secured with the same number of iron latches as the front doors.

"Tell me how you got out of that pickle?" I hear my sister's voice float out from the first room to my left, which is a dining room.

It's a deep, narrow room with more pine wood lining the walls and ceiling, matching every other room in this place. Instead of sconces on the walls, there's a small four-candle chandelier hanging from the center of the room, directly over the long dining table. Nina sits next to Maureen, who sits at the head of the table.

When they spot me, Nina pulls out the spindle-back dining chair next to her. The luxuries and fine furniture in this inn are like nothing I've seen before, especially out here where they lack resources.

As I sit down, I drag my fingers across the smooth, carved edge of the table and ask, "Did you bring this with you when you first came to Gravers Junction?"

"You can say something like that. But we also have an expert carpenter in town who enjoys making furniture." She then picks up a small silver bell and rings it. "So, how was your bath? Everything okay up there?"

"Yes, what happened?" Nina chimes in, abruptly shifting in her seat to face me. "We heard a loud noise and weren't sure if it was you or someone else."

Sheepishly smiling, I say, "Oh, I slipped getting out of the tub. Nothing hurt but my dignity." That last part isn't exactly a lie, since a stranger saw every curve of my bare body.

A petite woman with short brown hair enters the dining room, carrying a wooden tray that's nearly as large as she is. I jump up to help her with such a load, but the woman waves me to sit back down. I can't believe what I'm seeing as she balances the oversized tray with one hand. "You stay put right there," she says, her voice upbeat and brimming with energy. "I can handle it."

How can a person with a delicate frame hold so much weight on that massive tray without faltering? I watch in awe as the woman carefully sets the tray down at the other end of the table. Then, as she places our dinners in front of us—roasted chicken legs, mashed potatoes, and sliced carrots—she says, "It's nice to meet you both. I'm Ruby, and I oversee most of the gardening in town and all the cooking for the inn."

"Nice to meet you, Ruby," my sister says before turning her attention to the plate piled high with food. "I don't know what seasonings you use, but this smells amazing."

"Well," Ruby says as she returns to the tray to grab a basket of rolls, some butter, and a small jar of jelly, "if you're here long enough, I'd be happy to share some of my seasoning tips. I have a special closet where I dry out all of my herbs."

"That sounds wonderful," Nina says with delight. "Bex and I take turns cooking, and we aren't the most creative with tasty dinners."

Ruby sets the basket of rolls and condiments in front of us, and Maureen thanks the young woman before adding, "Is there any frozen cream left from last night?"

A wide smile spreads across Ruby's face. "Just enough for you three."

"Frozen cream? What's that?" I ask.

"It's a delicious cold treat that Ruby learned about from a friend who's traveled the world."

Nina stops spearing her carrots to ask, "Can I meet this friend of yours? I'd love to hear about their travels."

With a low chuckle, Ruby shakes her head. "Sorry, but she doesn't live in Gravers Junction. She usually comes through town once or twice a month."

"I think it's more than that," Maureen says with a snicker.

There's some unsaid inside knowledge being exchanged, but it doesn't seem relevant to our being here, so neither Nina nor I press for more details.

Ruby returns to her tray and grabs the decanter and three crystal wineglasses. She sets one glass in front of each of us, then pours the red wine about half full in each glass. When done, she sets the decanter off to the right of Maureen's plate.

"Will that be all?" Ruby asks, and when our host nods, Ruby picks up the enormous tray, gives us both a smile, and says, "I hope you'll consider staying for more than a day or two. We don't get too many outsiders, and it's always nice to meet and make new friends." To me, she adds, "If what Maureen said is true, that Persephone is truly gone, then we really could use your help in protecting…" Her voice trails off, and she looks to the older woman and then back to us. "Uh, protecting the people of Gravers Junction."

There seems to be a big secret about this town that people keep pausing about, as though they're avoiding telling us something. I don't press the topic, though. Instead, I say, "Oh, I'm no protector."

"We'll see about that." It's not Ruby but Maureen who answers. "Whether you remain here or return home, your life going forward will be that of a protector. We can at least offer you a roof over your head and food in your belly while you learn the laws of the land and train to master your abilities."

"Sounds like you're offering us a permanent place to stay," Nina asks with a mouthful of mashed potatoes.

"You'd be right in your assumptions. No one will ever force you to stay if you don't want to, and you'll always have a room here at Gravers Inn." She takes a long sip of wine before setting the crystal glass down. "The point is, you're a dustslinger now," she says to me. "If you've never thrown a punch or taken one, then you've got a lot to learn before you can stand on your own. And here's the best place to do it."

Pressing my palms flat against the table, I stare at my plate of food and say with disdain, "I didn't ask for this. I came here to tell you that woman's message, to get you to heal whatever this is she afflicted me with, and then go back to my normal, safe life."

Ruby takes her tray and quietly leaves while Maureen picks up her chicken leg and tears into it. After a few bites, she wipes the corners of her mouth and says, "You dwell too much on the past. You need to focus on the future. Your dustslinger powers aren't something you can simply get rid of."

There's that odd word again—dustslinger. And what does she mean by powers?

Anger and frustration simmer beneath my skin. Displeased with the unfolding conversation, I snap, my voice sharp, "That woman forced it out of her and into me! There has to be a way to get it out of me!"

"Her name was Persephone, and her magic is a part of you now. I don't even understand how she forced it out of herself and put it in someone else!" Maureen takes a deep breath and sips her wine. Then she calmly adds, "Please, sleep on it, deary. Decisions like this can't be made on a whim. Besides, I haven't even given you the grand tour of our quaint little town."

Nina and I share a defeated glance.

Before I can speak, our host says, "No more talk about staying or going. Let's finish our delicious supper. No need to let all this delicious food get cold."

Once our plates are empty, Ruby returns and clears the table. Then, shortly after, she brings us each a small bowl of this frozen cream. It's white like milk, but not drinkable. When she hands us some spoons, Nina doesn't hesitate to scoop some into her mouth. Her eyes close, and she sinks into her seat with a moan.

"This is the best thing I've ever tasted." Opening her eyes and going in for a second bite, she tells me, "Bex, you're going to love this."

"It tastes even better with apple pie," Maureen shares.

"That's right!" Ruby exclaims. "If you all decide to stay, we'll have a feast to celebrate, and I'll make extra frozen cream and plenty of pie."

I cut my spoon through the frozen cream, then lift it to my nose first. There's a strong hint of vanilla, which I love using when baking cookies. I put the spoonful in my mouth and slowly slide the metal utensil out while savoring the sweet, cold dessert. Nina was right. This is probably the best thing I've ever tasted. Before spooning up another bite, I can't help but suck the spoon, wanting to get every bit of frozen cream off. And, of course, as I'm sitting here sucking on a spoon, Garrett walks into the dining room. Our eyes briefly lock, and I quickly slip the spoon free of my mouth and set it on the table.

He clears his throat and looks to our host. "Everyone's inside and secure."

"Thank you." Then as he's turning to leave, Maureen calls for him to stay. "I believe I forgot to introduce you to our local sheriff, Garrett Redthorne. But no one calls him Sheriff, just Garrett."

"You're the local sheriff?" I almost choke on my question.

"Where's your badge?" Nina asks, still eating her frozen dessert. I swear she's about to lick the bowl like a famished canine.

He pulls out a silver badge hanging from a long thin chain, hidden beneath his shirt. There's some tarnish along one of the star spokes, and I'm guessing it's a hand-me-down. "It's not official like they do in your neck of the country," he explains. "But it's official enough for these parts."

Maureen rests her elbows on the table, wine glass in hand, as she says, "He's too modest, because everyone in Gravers Junction, and all throughout Graveyard Territory, knows that Garrett is the law around here. He and his deputies handle all kinds of *criminals* that need detaining. He and our deputies make sure the good folks of our little town are safe. In partnership with our local dustslinger, of course."

Garrett gives a curt nod to Nina, and then to me, but his attention doesn't linger too long on me. I imagine the embarrassment of earlier is still fresh in his mind. Where are his playful, inappropriate comments now, huh?

He tips his sunrider hat and says, "I'm heading to bed for the night. I'll catch you all in the morning." Then to Maureen, he adds, "I'll stay here tonight, if that's all right with you."

"Of course it is. Take 2B. Just remember to strip the bed in the morning."

"Yes, ma'am." And with that, he leaves us to our dessert.

"He's a good man. Never married. Close once, but…well, things weren't meant to be."

"That's a shame," Nina says. "He's handsome enough to catch any woman's attention where we're from."

Maureen smiles and nods. "If you stay, you'll learn quickly that this territory ain't like anywhere you're from or have visited. It's a game of survival out here, and love isn't always in the cards." She sinks into her chair and says, "It's almost as if there are forces at work out here that know when you've got something so valuable, taking it away will break you, making it easier to kill ya. And Garrett knows this. He ain't much of a gambling man and will chose duty over the risky business of love."

Nina pushes her empty bowl out of the way so she can rest her elbows on the table. "But you said he came close once."

She inhales a deep breath, as if that part of their lives is both good and hard to reminisce about. "It wasn't love, deary. Sure, they cared for one another a lot. But they were young, and everything is dire and world-ending when you're young. As adults, we have thicker skins, and most of us can recognize the signs of true love versus the illusion of it.

Physical attraction aside, it's a person's actions out in these parts that prove one's love. And Garrett had to learn that lesson the hard way."

"It's also about sacrifice and compromise." I'm not sure why I feel compelled to share, but reflecting on Levi makes me question whether our connection was genuine love or the fulfillment of a childhood dream. All I ever wanted was to marry a good man, own our own home and farm, have a family, and live a happy life. Isn't that love?

Maureen laughs. "You're not wrong, but that also tells me you haven't experienced the kind of love that drives a person mad. The kind of love that you think about every second of your day. The kind of love that drives your decisions, whether it's saving them or protecting them. It's not like the love of a friend or a sister. True love, or the love I'm talking about, is where you almost become two halves of one person. You work together for the same goals, while at the same time, you can't keep your hands off one another. You look into their eyes and you see a joy that you've never thought existed."

"You speak from experience," Nina says. "The heartache is still there, deep inside you."

Maureen wipes away a tear before it escapes. "Yes, deary. My late husband meant everything to me. I almost sacrificed the biggest prize in this territory to save him. But he wouldn't let me, and he sacrificed himself instead. This whole town feels his loss."

Something in me stirs with annoyance, and it's not the gritty sand along my skin. How dare she dismiss my loss as less important than hers. With a bitter tone, I tell the old woman, "I loved my husband. He was taken from me four years ago and…and I think about him every day."

"Is that so?" she asks, but I know she's not looking for further details. Resting her elbows on the table, she props her head on her folded hands. "Well, then you do have some experience with losing a loved one. I guess you're stronger than you look! If you can bear that kind of heartache and continue on living, then you're more of a fighter than you realize."

I'm not sure if she's being condescending or sincere, but either way, the annoyance has set in. I want to shout at her; I am broken. His absence has left me half a person. If it weren't for Nina moving in with me, I probably would've withered up and died on that farm all by myself. Then something hits me—was it dependency I missed or his company?

No, I loved my husband. I refuse to stain our marriage and what we had based on one woman's opinion of what love looks like. Instead of dwelling on how one measures love, I ask, "Mrs. O'Callaghan, will you please tell me more about what a dustslinger is?"

"Maureen is fine. You don't need all that Miss, Mrs., or Mister in this place. Things here need to be quick and accurate, otherwise people get hurt." I open my mouth to ask what she means, but she holds a hand up and beats me to it. "That might not make sense now, but it will in time. Now, I can't answer your questions about what exactly a dustslinger is—mainly because I don't know. Persephone was a locked vault when it came to her heritage, her powers, and her life outside of Gravers Junction. We knew little about her, but we all trusted her with our lives."

I lean into my chair. The curve of the spindle back gives me a slight hug. "So then who do I talk to about this dustslinging power?" The unfamiliar word stirs a ripple reaction down my arms from the sand.

"There is one person who knew Persephone well. Like, intimately well. I'll have Garrett take you out to see him tomorrow."

"We prefer to stay together, so I'll be accompanying them," Nina says with a finality in her tone.

"No, you won't. You'll stay here and help Ruby tend to the animals and the garden."

"We appreciate everything you're doing for us—giving us a room and feeding us the most delicious food—but you're not going to tell us where we can and can't go."

Maureen offers a kind smile, even though her words are anything but. "If you're not going to follow orders, then you get on your pretty little horse and hightail it home." Then she turns her attention to me. "But you, on the other hand. You aren't going anywhere until you understand what it means to be a dustslinger. Am I making myself clear?"

I reach for Nina's arm and gently squeeze it. To Maureen, I say, "We won't make trouble. And we appreciate your hospitality." Leaning closer to my sister, I whisper, "I'll be fine."

Nina doesn't break her stare from Maureen. The pleasantries they were exchanging moments ago have vanished. "I know you know what's out there. And I trust you'll keep my sister safe. But I'm gonna tell you right now if anything happens to her, you'll be the one to pay."

Maureen's lips curl into a wide smile. "Oh-wee. You're a fighter, aren't cha! I can't wait to see what you bring to the table when the time comes." After placing her napkin on the table, she stands and says goodnight. Before leaving the room, she says, "If you need anything, Garrett'll be on the second floor. And please, whatever you do, don't go outside." She looks at Nina. "Something tells me you already know that." In a lighter tone, she adds, "You won't want to sleep through Ruby's breakfast either. See you both in the morning."

When she's gone, I look to Nina and ask, "Was that a threat? Are we in danger here?"

"No, I don't think so. But you best take that firearm with you tomorrow, because she's not wrong about the evils out there. Me staying might be a good thing. I'll look around while you're out with," she bats her eyelashes, "the handsome town sheriff."

He is handsome. Though from what Maureen said, neither of us is looking to open our heart up to that kind of commitment. And I have no intention of letting myself get caught up in lustful temptations for a man who has sworn off love. Tomorrow, I plan to learn more about being a dustslinger and this territory, and what's got everyone so on guard. Maybe, along the way, I can start over with the sheriff and get better acquainted with him, in case we end up staying longer than planned. Yup, tomorrow should be an interesting day.

SIX

BEX

Exhausted, we head straight to bed after supper. The four-post bed is quite spacious, and its linens are incredibly soft, the finest I've ever experienced. What I wasn't expecting was how hot it gets up here on the third floor of the inn. Not needing the heavy quilt, Nina folded it up and laid it across the end of the bed before we settled for the night. My sister's a heavy sleeper…once she's out. Me, once I'm asleep, I'm usually out for the night, but getting to sleep doesn't always come easy. Like last night, while we slept out under the stars. I swear I was up for most of the night, worried about some wild dog or bandit sneaking up on us and killing us where we lay.

Here, though, I think I can't sleep because the weight of what to do is keeping my brain up and working. Stay…go…either way, it seems as if this skin condition isn't going anywhere.

After tossing and turning for what seems like hours, I toss off the sheet and slip out into the hallway. A little fresh air, and I bet I'll feel better and fall right asleep.

Reaching the second level, I pause and stare at 2B. The door's cracked open enough to see inside the room. I move closer and slowly push open the door. I'm not usually this intrusive, but there's something about this place that needs solving, and I aim to figure it out before I decide about staying or going.

The room's much smaller than ours with only a double bed and a dresser. On top of the dresser are a ceramic basin and a matching pitcher. In the middle of the bed, Garrett lies on his stomach. His arms reach up, tucking beneath his pillow. The top sheet has slipped down, resting just above his waist. He's shirtless, which doesn't surprise me since it's so damn hot in this inn. But what holds my attention are the long, thin lines scarring his right shoulder. There's another one lower, stretching across his lower back. That one's still pink along the edges, which could mean it's not new but not old either.

What caused such injuries? Knife fight? Maybe a fall, scraping along something sharp? Maybe that wolf isn't as domesticated as they thought. What kind of life are these people living out here?

When he stirs, lifting his head and repositioning it so he's now facing the other way, I freeze, praying to the gods that he doesn't wake and catch me standing here, watching him sleep. I should go, yet seeing a half-naked man confirms my earlier realization that I may be ready to experience a man's company again.

"What am I doing?" I whisper, knowing I'd be appalled if I discovered someone staring at my naked parts while sleeping, yet I can't turn away. My late husband had a moderate amount of body hair, leading me to believe most men were similar, but Garrett's skin is smooth, and his muscles are well-defined.

He stirs again, reaching behind him to lift the top sheet. This time, I don't gamble with him remaining asleep and quickly back out into the hall, pulling the door handle with me. My mistake is latching it closed. Not sticking around to find out if the *click* woke him, I hurry downstairs, through the main parlor, and into the back hall. I don't stop and go straight into the kitchen, where I find Ruby.

And Ruby is eating a sandwich while balancing an enormous axe on one finger. Startled by the scene before me, I stumble backward, hitting the door frame. "Oh, my apologies! I didn't mean to interrupt you."

"Ma'am!" Ruby scrambles to lower the axe, almost dropping her sandwich in the process. "I thought everyone was asleep." She rests the weapon against the legs of the table, apparently more worried about the mess of her sandwich. I take in the enormous axe, which isn't the normal wood-splitting kind, but rather an exquisite piece with oversized double blades and a thick handle, beautifully carved and polished. The quality of work is admirable, and the overall size is almost half of Ruby's height.

The kitchen is large enough to swallow her whole, axe and all. Two of the walls are stacked high with cupboards and shelves, and the others are lined with thick wood counters and iron stoves, the kind meant to feed many and often.

I slowly approach her, wanting to get a better look at the craftsmanship. "How are you able to balance something that big?"

A proud smile touches her lips as she picks up her treasured item and flicks it upward, keeping the toss low, just enough for the handle to spin back into her palm. She lifts it, running her hand over the smooth, carved handle.

"Oh, this old thing. Well, it belongs to my great-grandmother, Olivius 'the Bone-Crusher' Granitz."

"That's quite the name, *Bone-Crusher*," I softly echo. "I imagine there's a story behind that name?"

The petite woman shifts her gaze from her prized weapon to me, a smile spreading on her round face. "The tales I could tell you about her reign would keep us until next week."

"Where is she now?" Immediately after asking, I think about how old the woman must be if she's a great-grandmother. And then I feel terrible, a knot forming in my stomach, if I've accidentally brought up painful memories.

Setting the axe back down, leaning it against the long table centered in the kitchen space, she explains, "I don't know. I imagine she's out there somewhere. The last time I saw her was right before our homeland was attacked." Her sweet smile fades, and she picks up her sandwich, thick slices of pinkish meat hanging out the side. "That was a few years ago. Persephone found me wandering the Graveyard Territory and brought me here."

I slide onto a nearby stool to sit and listen to her story.

"I know I should go out and look for survivors, but I can't bring myself to do it. What if..." She pauses, staring at her sandwich, then slowly looks over at me. "What if I go home and everyone's dead, lying about? I don't want to see that."

Shaking my head, I agree, "No. No one would want to see that. There's no judgment here."

She takes a deep breath and nods, then takes a bite of her midnight snack. With a mouthful of meat and bread, she holds up her sandwich and mutters, "You want one?"

"No, thank you." I stand and move to the doorway. "What I need is some fresh air."

The short woman springs to her feet and hurries by me, blocking me from leaving the kitchen. "Whoa! You can't go outside. Not now. Not while it's dark."

"And why not?" I ask. "It's not like I'm going to wander off. I just need some fresh air."

"I know you're new and all, and I have a good inkling that Maureen is going to explain everything you need to know about surviving out here tomorrow, so for now, can you just take my word that going outside at night is a death sentence?"

"A death sentence!" I repeat. "That's absurd!"

"Where you're from, yes, it may be ridiculous. But out here, it's not. I swear on my gran-gran's axe." She holds up the giant axe and rests it back on one shoulder. The double-edge blades hang clear out into the hallway behind.

I step away and return to my seat on the stool. "Fine. Maybe I'll take you up on that sandwich."

"Now, you're thinking straight! One meaty sandwich coming up!"

SEVEN

BEX

Nothing exciting happens the next morning during breakfast. Ruby is bright-eyed and cheery as she sets out a morning feast that is, just as Maureen promised, delicious. I'm still in awe whenever I see her carrying that enormous tray, loaded with food or empty dishes.

Nina hasn't commented on Ruby's strength, which doesn't surprise me. My sister has been a slender twig for as long as I've known her, no matter how much she indulges in food. And food is her weakness. Nina has always enjoyed a good meal, and with the new varieties Ruby prepares, I imagine my sister's attention and excitement lie in exploring the edible delights. And like last night, Nina insists Ruby share all her recipes.

When done, Maureen offers to take us on a tour of the town. Both my sister and I finish our coffee, eager to learn more about what life is like in Gravers Junction.

It's another beautiful sunny day outside. There isn't a cloud in the sky. And to my surprise, there're folks out and about, working and talking like in any other town. Yesterday when we arrived, this place could easily have been mistaken for a ghost town. But not today. People are standing around talking and carrying baskets of food, while across the street, a group of men hammers boards over a broken picture window. With no form of signage except for the inn, there's no way to tell what's inside any of these buildings.

Maureen whistles, grabbing our attention. She proceeds along the boardwalk that connects to the adjacent building. Nina and I follow, our dress boots sounding much louder than Maureen's worn leather ones.

"There are no children." Nina leans closer and whispers behind one hand so only I can hear.

"Huh?"

"Where are all the kids?"

We continue to follow Maureen out into the middle of the dirt road that cuts straight through town, and Nina's right—there isn't a single child running around or following the skirt of a mother.

Before I can inquire, Maureen stops and says, "You won't find another town like Gravers Junction anywhere else in the world. I can guarantee you that." She turns, facing back toward the inn, but points to the building next to it and then drags her finger through the air, pointing to the other four buildings that follow. Lush grass occupies the narrow gaps between the structures.

"All those buildings there…well, they aren't real."

Her last word catches me off guard. "Real?" I repeat, unsure if I heard her correctly. At the same time, Nina asks, "What do you mean, 'they aren't real'? Like you can't go inside?"

"Oh, you can go inside, but they aren't trading posts or service buildings. You see," she says, walking over to the single-story building closest to the inn, "we don't get many travelers passing through town needing supplies or looking to send a post."

"I can believe that," I say as we step into a small front room. There's nothing in it but a few chairs and an old leather trunk tucked under the window…then it hits me that the window inside isn't the same size as the one on the outside. I go back out, measure it with my eyes, and return. There is no doubt that the interior window is much smaller.

"What's going on here?" I ask, pressing a hand to the front wall that's covering the picture window. A rectangle cutout sits right where the full window should be. I can see outside through it, but it's barely wide enough for both Nina and me to look through.

Maureen comes over and lifts a hanging doorway on hinges and then locks it into place, covering up the cutout completely. It's a lookout. She knocks a curved knuckle on the front wall and adds, "We fortified the walls with hammered-out sheets of iron."

"What does that even mean?" Nina asks, mimicking Maureen and knocking on the wall.

"It means there're basically two walls here, and between them are sheets of iron metal."

I make a guess as to why, and say, "Bullets, right? To keep them from getting inside."

Maureen nods. "And so far, it's worked. We got really lucky in finding this smithy guy. His ideas are far beyond anything I've ever seen."

Looking about the room, I ask, "What's behind the closed door?"

"Come on, I'll show you." She's a hard walker as her boots pound against the floorboards across the room. She lifts the iron latch, and we make our way into the back room. There's another cutout at the back, with a chair next to it. There's also a small table with two chairs off to the side. What throws me is the staircase leading underground.

I walk over and stare down. "I've seen underground cellars where people keep food from spoiling, but they're never inside a home."

Maureen comes over next to me. "It doesn't lead to a cellar. And it's the only way we stay safe from the evils out there." She gestures with a nod to the front of the building. "If you want to survive Graveyard Territory, then you've got to adapt to the land. And here, the land doesn't provide trees, rivers, or mountains—only the earth beneath our feet."

Without another word, she disappears down the stairs. I'm about to go down too when I notice Nina staring at the stairwell opening and shaking her head. I hurry over to her and cup her shoulders. "What's wrong?"

Her trembling gaze drifts from its target to me. "There's something powerful down there, Bex. Maybe you're right. Maybe we shouldn't get mixed up in whatever these people are fighting."

"Maybe," I say, giving her some reassurance that I haven't settled on what I want to do. "You know that this is something we both have to agree on, right? Staying here doesn't only affect me, but you too. And we'll make that choice together, when the time comes."

She gives me a small smile. "Thank you."

I pull her in for a hug. Then after, I say, "So if you want to leave, then we'll leave. But I am curious to know exactly what's going on here. What secrets does this town hide?"

She nods, and we head down the stairs. At the bottom, Maureen holds open a large wooden door reinforced with iron cross plates.

When we reach the bottom, I'm once again taken aback. There's a long, wide hallway stretching out in both directions, to our left and right. The walls and ceiling are tightly lined with the same pine planks as inside the inn. Thick support beams are embedded in the walls and ceiling every ten or fifteen paces, with lanterns hanging like sconces on the walls. The warm light brightens this underground passage.

Two metal pipes run the length of the hall, snug against the ceiling on opposite walls. One is copper, the other a slightly larger cast iron pipe.

"What are those?" I ask, pointing to the two metal pipes.

"Observant. Good. And I'll get to those soon. Right now, come along." Maureen waves for us to keep up.

Her brisk pace has us moving quickly down the hall, which is unfortunate because I want to explore and see what all's down here. We pass several closed doors on both sides of the hall. One door is open, and I can't resist stopping to peek inside.

There's a small cold wood stove, a table with two chairs, a waist-height bookcase full of books, and a full-size cabinet. The lantern hanging on a hook over the table is dark, so I push the door open more, letting more light from the hall inside. From out of the shadows, at the back of the room, a door frame reveals itself. Through it, is the faint outline of a bed.

"This is where you all live? Underground?" I ask, shouting loud enough for Maureen to hear me.

She and Nina have gotten away from me, but not out of sight. Maureen waves to me and shouts, "Yes, yes, now hurry and come here!"

I leave the door open and hurry toward them. Maureen climbs another set of stairs, and Nina's trailing behind. I gather my skirt in my hands and follow. When we reach the top, Maureen's standing in a storage room filled with crates, barrels, potato sacks, brooms, and even a few weapons. She opens the door and gestures for us to look. Nina steps out first, and I follow to see we're now standing in the back hall of the inn. The kitchen is straight across from us, where Ruby is washing the dishes from breakfast.

"Do all the buildings connect?" I ask, glancing back at the stairs.

"Aye, they do," Maureen says with a proud smile. "And not just this side of town. You can get to the other buildings too."

"That must've taken years to dig out." I move over to the stairs, ready to go back down and explore more of what they've built underground.

"Hold on there," Maureen says, shaking a hand to me. "There's plenty of time to explore down there. What I want to show you next is outside." She turns and walks out into the parlor room, and Nina shrugs before turning on her heels to see what Maureen wants us to see next.

Ruby steps out of the kitchen, drying off her hands on a dishrag, and says, "Oh, I think I'll come with ya. She's going to show you my favorite part of town."

We follow Maureen and my sister, who are now standing outside. The townsfolk are bustling about, and yet still no children. I spot the two men from yesterday, the father-son duo, and they're talking with Garrett.

His eyes are hooded by the wide brim of his dark brown leather sunrider. The edges are worn and slightly curved at the sides. The long sleeves of his shirt are rolled up to his elbows. In one hand, he clutches a blue cloth handkerchief. I think about the injuries he's hiding beneath that shirt. With everything we've seen so far, and the scars I saw last night while he lay in bed, the weight of this place settles in—we could die out here if we stay. This place is all about surviving to live one more day.

Is that the kind of life I want to live?

And would I stay if Nina didn't want to? There's a power here that has her unnerved, and it wouldn't be right for me to ask her to stay if she didn't want to.

With metal sheets between walls, not going out after dark, and living underground, I'm starting to believe the rumors people say about Graveyard Territory. Then, to add to it all, they expect me to be some kind of dustslinging protector.

It's only morning, and I already know I'm going to need another relaxing hot bath tonight. I look to Garrett again, still talking with those men, and think how I'll be locking the bedroom door before my bath.

He stands there, so confidently, listening to the two other men talk, arms crossed, focused on them. And then, he's not focused on them…but on me. He finds me staring back, standing in the middle of the dirt road while Maureen, Nina, and Ruby make their way along a stone path between two buildings.

Garrett tips his hat forward, which causes the two men he's talking with to turn and look my way. The sudden onslaught of attention snaps me from my reverie, and I hurry to find the others. I keep my gaze to the ground, and don't give the men a second glance.

The three buildings in the middle are smaller structures, while the large building at the town's entrance is set a good ten feet from the rest. The last building—the oversized barn—is long, almost twice the size of the three in the middle combined. Nina waves to me from the closest barn door, which is pushed open. The door frame could easily fit a carriage through it.

"This is their barn!" she says excitedly. "Maureen says they have to lock up everything inside each night, so they built a barn big enough to house every animal, every carriage, and all the hay and animal feed. It's quite impressive."

And she's right. The exterior is quite misleading. Inside, stalls and pens are laid out at the far end, with a small corral space in the center. The opposite end, where we stand, holds two carriages, a stagecoach, and an open carriage with a buckboard driver's bench and an open back. All the farming tools are kept organized, either hanging on the wall or stacked neatly on shelves fixed to the walls. There's even stuff stored up in the rafters. And I spot a loft area at the other end with a ladder hiding in the corner.

"This is extraordinary," I say, taking in as much as I can.

"Well, we do what we can to make sure the animals are protected." Maureen picks up a bucket half full of cracked corn and carries it to the open back door. "Come on, let's feed the chickens."

"Oh, you're going to love it out here!" Ruby says, looping her arm through mine.

It's not the number of chickens or the sizable garden area growing in the back that steals my attention, but the giant cage they've built over the entire outdoor space. Everything is contained within the enclosed space. And as dividers, they've incorporated waist-height wood fencing to separate the chickens, pigs, and sheep from Ruby's garden area. The exterior cage—the walls and ceiling—is constructed out of chicken-wire fencing.

"Is this so the animals don't run off and get lost in the prairie?" I ask, taking in the elaborate caging system they've created.

"It's mostly to keep things from getting in, but also because there's no sunlight underground. We had to come up with a way to grow our food and let the animals get some fresh air, while being smart about where we live and the threats out there." Ruby turns and holds a hand over her eyes, shielding the rising sun. She then quickly adds, "And we've rigged it so that at night we can charge the metal, making it so anyone who touches the fencing gets shocked, like if lightning were to strike them."

Ruby's grin clearly expresses how proud she is of what she's done here. I can't help but admire her skill and innovation about the way she's protecting the animals and her garden.

Both my sister and I turn to the closest section of chicken-wire fencing and approach it. Ruby comes up from behind and grabs it, her fingers clasping between different sections of the chicken wire. "It's not on right now. I'll charge the cage right before the sun sets."

"Because we stay inside after dark," I say, repeating what Ruby told me during our midnight conversation.

"That's right," Maureen confirms, grabbing a tin bucket full of cracked corn. "Going outside after dark is dangerous. You run the risk of something evil catching ya."

I'm not exactly sure I want to know, but I ask anyway, "What kind of evil? Unlawful bandits? Wild dogs?"

"Maybe, but I'm talking about the kind you didn't even know existed. The kind that you'd only think existed in your nightmares."

Nina's hand slips into mine. "And these are the monsters you're expecting my sister to fight?"

With a doubtful raise of her brows and a sigh, Maureen says, "Yes. Though, you both look like the only thing you've ever punched is a bowl full of rising dough."

That's an excellent point. I wouldn't even know how to throw a punch, or dodge one for that matter. The thought of being assaulted has me inhaling deeply, anticipating what the pain might be like. Our cow accidentally knocked me over, and I landed hard on my backside, and that bruise was so painful I could barely sit for over a week. I could only imagine the bruising from an attack would feel much worse.

"You're much stronger than you think, physically I mean." Maureen tosses some of the feed out onto the patchy grass where the chickens congregate. More of them come running out from inside the coop, eager to get their morning breakfast. When done, she continues with her explanation, saying, "Well, Persephone was strong, and fast, and most folks around here fear and respect her for what she does…I mean, did…for those of us who needed protecting. Even the evil out there knew that going up against her wouldn't end in their favor. So, wherever she went, evil avoided her or complied and did as she asked."

"I can't imagine I'd ever get that level of respect from anyone," I murmur, wondering what it would be like for people to fear me.

Maureen dumps the rest of the cracked corn out and sets the pail down. "You will, if you choose to embrace the power and magic within you."

"Magic?" I ask, glancing at Nina.

"Yes, yes." She waves a hand through the air like it's nothing. "Magic exists, along with other things. I don't really know how to explain it, so don't ask. And I don't know the different kinds. That's a question for Ruby's friend next time she visits town."

"Two weeks!" Ruby shouts over from where she's got one leg stretched out into her garden and she's reaching for something behind a tall, leafy plant stalk. "She'll be here in a couple of weeks, if I've been counting my days right."

Maureen chuckles, then shouts to Ruby, "Looking forward to having her!" She resumes her chores and picks up another bucket. This one contains food scraps from the kitchen. Facing the pen near the chickens, she clicks her tongue. Two large pigs and three pink piglets come rushing over as Maureen dumps the contents into their trough. Looking at us, she asks, "So, do you want to see more, or are you thinking you might cut and run?"

"More, please," we both say in unison. Hearing Nina agree eases my guilty thoughts about considering the idea of staying.

"Good," she says with a smile. "I've got to take care of a few things, so why don't you two go and get your horses and bring them out into the corral for a bit. I'm sure they'd like some fresh air." Before she heads off, she adds, "Oh, and Bex. You and Garrett will head out to visit Persephone's friend within the hour."

I nod, nervous and excited to be seeing more of this territory.

After parting ways, leaving Ruby to her garden, we head back inside the barn. The horse stalls are at the other end, and as we walk, I take in the overwhelming scale of how big and long this barn is. They aren't kidding about locking everything up inside at night.

We find our horses together in the same stall, nibbling on fresh hay. It's nice to see Tumbleweed, and Nina goes straight to Frostbite.

"This place is pretty amazing. Not what I was expecting," Nina confesses, slipping the horse's halter over Frostbite's head. I do the same with Tumbleweed before attaching the lead line. We walk the horses out the open end of the barn where there are multiple corrals. A beautiful black mare is in the one closest to the barn.

"I wouldn't put your horses in there with her," Garrett says, coming up from behind us. He and a young man, maybe in his late teens, head toward the black mare. "Davie, make sure that gate is locked. We can't have her getting out again."

"Yes, sir!" Davie says, pulling out his gloves from his back pocket.

Garrett gestures to the second corral. "Let's put them in this one." He unlatches the lock and opens the gate. Nina goes first with Frostbite.

I offer a polite, "Thank you," while following my sister into the enclosed area.

He locks the gate and walks over to Davie, who is leaning against the wooden fence and watching the mare.

Releasing Tumbleweed from the lead rope, she explores the area with Frostbite. I ask Nina, "So what do you think of that garden and pen area?"

She shrugs one shoulder. "This whole place is an oddity. People living underground and them putting a cage around their gardens and animals, I think it has something to do with whatever power I keep sensing beneath the earth. They're hiding something, and we can't decide until we know what it is."

I nod, inhaling a deep breath. The tall grass out in the prairie covers the land surrounding the town. It's just tall grass and sky for miles. "It's not just secrets here in town we gotta figure out, but whatever's out there too."

"Yeah," she says with a somber tone. "I'm not sure I want to know what's out there."

Garrett's shouting something, drawing my attention to where he and Davie are trying to corner that mare. I tell Nina, "I'll be right back."

I rest my arms up on the top rail of the corral fence and watch the two men. When they finally get the bridle over its head, they quickly back off, letting the horse get used to the head equipment.

"You breaking that horse in?" I ask.

Garrett tells Davie something I can't hear before walking over to me. The corner of his mouth curls up into a welcoming smile, stirring a pleasant warmth in my belly.

"Nah. She's broken already, just not keen on her new home yet."

"Where'd she come from?" Curiosity has me wondering not only about the horse, but more about who this man is.

He reaches the fence and comes right up to it, propping an elbow mere inches from where my arms rest. "Let's just say I won her in a poker game."

"Sheriff, I swear Maureen said you weren't a gambling man."

He briefly looks away before softly chuckling and saying, "There's a lot about me, ma'am, you don't know."

"I reckon you're right. But I'd like for us to be friends, as long as you keep that cheeky tongue in check."

This has him laughing. "I can't make any promises, but I'll try, ma'am."

Lowering my arms from the railing, I say, "First, you don't have to call me 'ma'am.' I'd actually prefer if you don't. It makes me sound old, and though I'm not a youth, I don't feel like a ma'am."

"My apologies. I thought I'd overheard you saying you were married last night, during supper."

Now it's my turn to smile big. "Eavesdrop much?" I ask.

He takes off his sunrider hat and runs a hand through his pale brown hair. "No, ma'am—sorry, no, I happened to be in the kitchen."

"Ah, well." My gaze drifts from him to the black mare. "I was married. But he was taken from me." After a brief silence, I looked at him again. "Now, it's me and my sister tending to the farm."

"I'm sorry for your loss."

"Thank you. Though it was four years ago. And fairly early in our marriage." Then I quickly add, as if my words could be misinterpreted, "That doesn't mean we didn't love one another."

"Of course. I wouldn't dare to assume you weren't. Can I ask what happened?" He slipped his hat back onto his head, the wide brim casting a shadow over the top part of his face.

Shaking off the momentary lapse of embarrassment, I explain, "I don't know what happened. I'd been visiting my parents, who live about an hour south of our farm, and when I came back…well, there was blood and the local sheriff explained Levi had been killed in a random act of violence. Wrong place at the wrong time, kind of situation. They buried my husband out in the field, and so all I'd left of him was his gravestone."

"That's horrible. No one should have to come home to that kind of news."

"No. They shouldn't."

"So, what would you like me to call you?" he asks, his kind smile returning.

"Oh, I guess I'd forgotten to introduce myself to you last night." I hold out a hand, and he takes it, shaking it gently. He doesn't shy away from a firm grip, giving me the same respect I assume as if he were to shake a man's hand. Or maybe he just wants to hold my hand and not let go. Either way, the contact has my stomach fluttering again.

"Rebecca Rose Ellington. But everyone calls me Bex."

"Well, then I shall call you Bex too. Is Ellington your maiden name or married name?"

"So many questions. Am I under investigation for something, Sheriff?"

This makes him laugh. "Now look who's being cheeky. And no." His voice gets deeper, and he explains, "I'm hoping to get to know you better, that's all. You and your sister." He steps back and looks over to where Nina is brushing Frostbite. "Especially if you're planning on moving to town."

"Oh, we haven't made any final decisions regarding moving out here, not yet."

His smile falters, and then he locks his gaze onto mine. "Good. Don't make any hasty decisions without knowing exactly what you're getting yourselves into. Even if that means staying an extra few days. Just please know what you're getting into before committing." He swallows, and the bulge in his throat bobs. "It may seem like a simple life out here, but it ain't. There's nothing easy about living out here in Graveyard Territory."

There's a heavy weight to his advice, and I don't ignore it. He's being honest without divulging whatever it is he fears.

"They're ready for you, Garrett!" Davie calls from the threshold of the open barn doors.

Garrett inhales a deep breath, and then says, "You should say goodbye to your sister. We won't be back until tomorrow."

I nod and push off the fence and make my way over to Nina. Let's hope we don't run into any of these evil dangers Maureen and Garrett keep insisting will get us if we go outside after dark. And if we do, will I be able to call on my dustslinging powers to fight? Or will I be one of those poor souls who ends up dead out in Graveyard Territory, another body for the earth to claim.

I think we're instinctively born to fight for our lives.

The fear most people have is losing or dying because of inadequate strength or an inability to defend themselves. I know I do. But what if I had strength and power, like Maureen said? And all I need is to learn how to wield it and how to fight back. Would that be enough for me to embrace this life?

I think it just might be.

EIGHT

BEX

The cabin of the stagecoach I'm sitting in is lacking any means of comfort, and without a designated road, the uneven earth has me bouncing in my seat. Garrett said the ride would be about four hours, and he insisted we needed the wagon to bring this man, Booker I believe his name was, supplies.

When we hit a deep hole along the plains, I almost fall right off the bench and onto the flour sacks and potatoes piled up on the seat across from me. They secured some crates to the roof and luggage hold in the rear, but what was left ended up in the cabin.

"Sorry about that!" Murphy shouts from the buckboard seat where he and Garrett sit. Murphy, a sheriff's deputy, is also Davie's father. They're the father-son pair I've seen a couple times now in town.

I pick my hat up off the floor and set it on the seat again. I wanted to ride Tumbleweed alongside, but Garrett wouldn't have it. He insisted that it would be safer for me to ride in the stagecoach. Their horses knew the way home if things got ugly and he had to let them run free. I didn't want to imagine what that might entail, so I didn't argue. But it still rubbed me the wrong way. If I'm meant to be some kind of protector, he needs to let me experience this land—the good and the ugly.

There's a part of me that is upset I had to make this trip sitting inside the cabin all alone, with no one to talk to. Why didn't Maureen let Nina come? Her company would've helped keep my boredom at bay. There's only so much open prairie one can admire before the thrill fades and boredom sets in.

"We're about there!" Murphy shouts. Davie, who's usually right by Murphy's side, stayed in Gravers Junction to help fix a broken ladder somewhere…or something like that. I wonder where the boy's mother is. He might be the youngest person in Gravers Junction. Unless Maureen is hiding the children underground somewhere.

Off in the distance, a strange rock formation sits along the horizon. It appears massive, taller than the Gravers Inn. The red surface is smooth—well, it looks smooth from here. The natural formation is so out of place with the flat plains stretching out for as far as the eye can see. It's as if the gods themselves carefully arranged these massive narrow boulders against one another like a giant campfire for them to sit around and tell ancient stories. It's quite beautiful, and I hope we get a closer look at it before heading back to town.

I'm so enamored of the rock formation off in the distance that I don't notice out the other side that we've come upon a small cabin. There's a sizable barn too, attached to the back side of the home. Normally, barns are set a good distance from any farmhouse, but out here in Graveyard Territory, I've learned that it's not safe to go outside at night, and if you need to get to another building, you have to either build them on top of one another, or have an underground tunnel connecting them.

The second the stagecoach stops, a man sitting in a rocker on the front porch stands and makes his way to us. A pair of hunting hounds leap to their feet and flank the man's sides.

"I wasn't expecting you until next week," he shouts, looping his thumbs through the front of his suspenders. "Your order isn't ready. Maybe tomorrow, after tonight's full moon."

Garrett hops down from the bench seat where he and Murphy sit. Murphy does the same, but on the other side. Garrett says to the man, "Not here for that, but good to know," while Murphy opens the door for me and says, "Don't wander off. The snakes are poisonous in these parts, you hear me?"

I nod and climb out, grabbing my hat before Murphy shuts the door. The muscles in my legs are ready to stretch and shake off the lingering stiffness. Bright, warm sunlight claims every part of the open land. I put on my sunrider and tighten it by sliding the bead up the leather straps. My pale blue dress grazes the red dirt of the man's plot, and I'm thankful the sand sensation beneath my long sleeves remains dormant. No danger here.

I circle around the back while Murphy climbs up onto the tread step to unload the bags and crates secured on the roof. The man, Booker, is facing away from me, and the second

Garrett's gaze finds me from over the man's shoulder, he turns. The man's eyes narrow for a brief second before he removes his hat and brushes a hand through his overgrown dark locks, peppered with streaks of gray. He holds his sunrider hat to his chest and takes a step closer.

"Well, hello there. I'm Booker. And you are?" His smile is kind, and his teeth are abnormally white. Maybe the whitest teeth I've ever seen. He catches me staring and brings the tips of his fingers over his mouth. "Oh, don't mind my pearly whites. I'm quite particular about keeping them clean," he says with a wink.

There's something about him that unsettles me, yet the dustslinger powers aren't stirring.

"I was admiring your smile, and my name is Rebecca Rose Ellington, but everyone calls me Bex."

Booker brushes his hair back once more before setting his wide-brimmed sunrider hat on his head. "And what might be the purpose of this unexpected, yet lovely, out-of-the-blue visit?"

"Book, we've got some bad news and, well, some good news," Garrett says, stepping around so he's included in the conversation.

"Is that right? Well, let's have the good news first, then we can deal with the bad." The two hound dogs, with their oversized floppy ears and long snouts, have already lain together in the red dirt. One watches us closely while the other keeps an eye on the open land.

"I've come into some special powers that I need your help to understand," I answer, not wanting to be the one to dish out the bad news.

Booker looks from Garrett to me. "All right, show me where you got bitten."

"Bitten?" I ask, my body tensing at his assumption. Did she bite me? Was that how she transferred her powers to me? I think back to that stormy night, and there was no way she had the strength to do anything but lie in my arms and die. Most of her energy was spent on gasping for air and getting me to remember her message.

"Tell Maureen O'Callaghan Persephone is dead. Tell her it was Malik Graves. Say the name!" the woman in my arms yells, spitting up blood. Her lips were coated in red as she yelled over and over, "Say his name!"

"Mal-Malik Graves," I stutter.

"Good," she says with a long sigh, sinking into my lap. Her breathing was more labored. "Gravers Junction." Another shallow breath. "Persephone is dead." Her eyes fluttered closed.

Our hands were clasped tightly over her chest, and I could feel her breathing grow weaker and weaker. Then, as she spoke her last words, "Malik Graves," a whirlwind of sand swept in through the open back door and circled around us like a twister. I held on to the woman's body, as if to protect her from the tornado of dirt, sand, and dust, only to be struck in the head by something hard. I swore as I blacked out, my mouth filled with sand and dust as the cyclone spun around us.

The one blessing that night was that Nina wasn't home. She was visiting our parents a few hours south. When she returned, every surface within our kitchen was covered in dirt, and not just a dusting but buckets of the stuff.

"I wasn't bitten," I clarify at the same time Garrett says, "It's not like that. It's a different kind of magical power—one you're familiar with someone else having."

Still focused on what he meant by getting bitten, I open my mouth to ask what power comes from a bite, but then Booker says her name and I quickly refrain from asking.

"Persephone."

Garrett nods.

Booker looks at me, eyeing my arms and hands. "You're a dustslinger?"

"Apparently," I confirm with a shrug. A trickle of sweat breaks loose and trails the skin along my spine, and I can't tell whether it's from nerves or from the heated day. It gets fairly hot out in these parts, especially when there's no overcast.

A smile spreads and he rubs the back of his neck. "Well, damn. Persephone will be thrilled to meet ya, though she's not here right now. I'm not sure when she'll—"

"Booker," Garrett cuts in, his voice low, and the sorrow laced in it mirrors the look in his eyes, "Persephone isn't coming."

The man purses his lips and stares at the ground. After a moment, he shakes his head. "Nah. Whatever you're about to say, it's not true. She's a fighter. That woman can get out of any pinch she faces." He pushes past Garrett and walks toward his cabin, whistling for his hounds to follow, and they do.

"Booker!" Garrett calls after the man.

Murphy comes around carrying a stack of crates. "You two should go talk with him. I'll get all this unloaded and into his barn."

Garrett nods and gestures with a tilted head for me to go

first. The man's front door is open, so we follow him inside. It's a cozy cabin with an open living space, a bedroom in the back corner, and then a door that I assume leads to the barn. There's a second door between the barn door and the bedroom doorway, and I'm tempted to see what's behind it. A washroom or a storage room, perhaps.

Booker sighs, hanging his sunrider hat on a wooden peg stuck into the wall at eye level. He's muttering curses and when he finally faces us, he looks right at Garrett and asks, "Are you sure?"

"She died in my arms," I explain. "I don't know how she found her way to my farm, because we live out in Billingsworth County, but she showed up in the middle of the night, bleeding out from multiple gunshot holes in her chest."

"Dammit, Persephone!" Booker seethes, kicking a nearby wooden chair. Upon hitting the wall, the seat breaks, sending splinters of wood flying. My heart beats faster, unsure if I should wait outside or stay and give the man a moment to calm down.

"I swear I'm gonna find out who did it and then run that son of a bitch through."

"That's your business," Garrett chimes in. "But right now, somehow, Persephone gave her dustslinger powers to Bex, and she needs help to understand how to..."—he glances over at me—"to access them."

Wiping his nose with the sleeve of his shirt, Booker paces the space for a few more moments, before stopping and letting out a frustrated sigh. His eyes glisten with tears as he shakes his head at me. "I can't help you. She never told me about how it all works. There's some kind of loyalty pact or secret oath that prevents her from talking about the inner workings of a dustslinger."

That makes sense. Knowing the source of her magic would allow her enemies to easily discover her vulnerabilities. That might've even been the reason for her death that evening—someone discovered a way to skirt her defenses.

But then I focus on the other part of Booker's words. The part about a loyalty pact or secret oath. "If she wasn't permitted to talk about her powers, that must mean there're more out there, right?"

Booker clears his throat, and despite still being upset, he composes himself, which I believe is for our benefit. He crosses his arms over his broad chest and says, "Well, if there are, we've never seen 'em. The only dustslinger I've ever known is Persephone."

"That doesn't change the fact that there may be others out there," I retort.

The two men don't answer. Instead, Booker raises an eyebrow at Garrett and says, "It's a full moon tonight."

"No." Garrett waves his hands, crossing his arms in a *no* gesture. "It's too risky."

"What's too risky?" I ask, but the men continue plotting a course without me.

"It's the only way to get the answers you're looking for." Booker points a finger at me but speaks to Garrett. "Only those born of the veil heritage have the natural connection. The rest of us have to present ourselves and be judged...if we want her ear and guidance."

"Who?" I've had about enough of this speaking around me.

"Isn't there another way?" Garrett asks, still disregarding my presence.

"Once word gets out that Persephone's gone," Booker's tone is concerning, "Gravers Junction's gonna be getting a lot of unwanted visitors. Even more if they discover you've got a virgin dustslinger."

"Virgin?" I repeat with a harsh tone and a crazed woman's hand clap. This has the two men turning their gazes on me.

Garrett shakes his head and clarifies, "No. Not like that. He just means you haven't been acquainted with…oh, forget it. You wouldn't understand."

"And I won't ever understand if you two keep dodging my questions! Now tell me. Who must I become acquainted with in order to learn more about my dustslinger powers?"

"Before you jump in and agree to what's being suggested"—Garrett lets out a frustrated groan and looks to me—"you should know that Booker lives out here for two reasons."

Booker cuts in to finish explaining, "The first is because I'm a werewolf, hence the pearly whites being so immaculate."

My gaze goes wide to their fullest as I look him over. "That's not possible. Werewolves aren't real."

"I assure you, ma'am, we're real. I'm also an alpha, and I chose not to have a pack. Too much responsibility. I prefer the loner life. But there are packs out there, some more organized than others."

I look to Garrett and ask, "Is this why it's not safe to go outside at night?"

He nods and adds, "Among other things."

Maureen's earlier mention of things out there that only exist in nightmares resurfaces in my mind. "Other things? What other things?" I can't decide whether I want to have Garrett take me back to town so Nina and I can pack up and leave this delusional place or if I want to stay and learn all there is to know.

I take a deep breath.

Werewolves are real.

I stare at the man before me. He looks so…normal. When Garrett doesn't answer my question about *other things*, I turn to Booker. "Is that why you asked me if I'd gotten bitten?"

He nods, and then sighs with an apologetic smile. "There's a lot of things out here in Graveyard Territory that can't be explained, darlin'. If you're originally from Billingsworth, then I recommend you think long and hard about staying in these parts. Billingsworth is a safe place to live, no aberrants out there."

"What's an aberrant?"

"You are. I am." Booker looks to Garrett, then says, "And—"

"And that just means there's more to you than being human," Garrett finishes for his friend. "Whether it's magic that makes you one of the branded aberrants, or if you're born into one of the races."

I lower myself into one of the wooden chairs. "So, there's other kinds of creatures that exists? Ones I only thought were from story books?"

"We don't like the word *creatures*. Aberrants is the universal name that separates us from the humans," Booker explains. Rolling up his sleeve, he shows me his branded mark. It's exactly like the one I saw on my back through the reflection of the handheld mirror.

Reaching one hand over my shoulder, I try and touch the spot where it's scarred into my skin. Garrett tilts his head, as if he's piecing together what I'm doing. "I'm sorry about this, Bex. You didn't ask for this, and now you're kind of stuck with it."

"Hey, why was Persephone out in Billingsworth County anyway?" Booker stares at me, as if I know why she was at my farm.

"She didn't say. Before she passed, she gave me a message to give to Maureen." They both stare at me, waiting for me to relay the message. "Oh, sure. Why the hell not." The curse feels good on my tongue. "She said to tell Maureen that Persephone is dead and that Malik Graves did it."

"It *was* him! That son of a bitch!" Booker punches the wall, and it goes straight through, leaving a giant hole to the outside.

"Listen," I say, getting to my feet, hoping to elevate some of his heartache. "I want to do her right and be the best dustslinger I can be to protect myself and those around me— whether it be at Gravers Junction or if we decide to return home. So, whatever dangerous thing we need to do in order for me to learn more about whatever's inside me, let's do it."

Booker flexes his hand, the cuts along his knuckles from punching the wall slowly heal right before my eyes. Well, damn. Taking a step closer, he tells me, "The Spirit of the Land knows all, and she's the only one who can bring you closer to the answers you seek."

"This is a bad idea," Garrett grumbles. "The spirit isn't always kind, and if she deems you unworthy, she'll claim your soul and leave your body to decay and return to the earth it came from."

I blink before wrinkling my nose at him. "Well, that sounds unpleasant."

Garrett dips his gaze and stares me right in the eyes. "I need you to fully understand what you're agreeing to. This is dangerous, and you could die."

The silence that fills the room is unsettling. I want to do whatever's necessary, yet I'm scared that if things go wrong, I may never see another day again.

"How about I cook us up some stew for supper while y'all think about it? We've got time," Booker says, shoving an old shirt into the hole he's put in the wall. "We wouldn't be able to call on her until midnight anyhow."

I roll up my sleeves, not worried if the dustslinger within me comes to life. Booker knows my secret. "How can I help?" I ask, and he hands me a knife.

"You can cut up the vegetables, and I'll go get us some meat."

"I'll go find Murphy," Garrett grumbles, clearly annoyed.

If what they're saying is true, and this Spirit of the Land can claim my soul, ending my life, I regret not arguing more with Maureen about letting my sister accompany me on this trip. What if I die tonight, leaving Nina alone in this world? Straightening my shoulders and grabbing a potato, I refuse to think any other thoughts but positive ones. I will see Nina again. I will conquer this challenge. Tonight is not the night I die.

NINE

NINA

Ruby finds me sitting outside and hands me a plate. The pot roast super she's prepared smells amazing, and even though I'm supposed to be pouting about not being allowed to travel with Bex, I take the bowl and savor each bite. We sit outside at a long wood table with benches rather than chairs. It's situated behind the inn, over by the large oak tree. Ruby doesn't eat, but she does sit and keep me company. While I eat, she remains silent, staring out into the open plains.

I set my plate down on the ground, leaving a small portion for the shaggy dog that's been keeping us company.

"What's his name?" I ask, finally breaking the silence.

She licks her spoon and looks at the dog. "I think it's Gopher. He showed up one day, and took a liking to Davie. The boy's been taking care of him, bringing him food and giving him shelter down below at night."

A whistle comes from across the street behind us, and Ruby and I turn to see Davie standing outside one of the smaller buildings. "Gopher!" he hollers, and the dog sprints away.

"He's a friendly pup, and good for announcing strangers."

I recall when Bex and I first arrived in town, we'd heard him barking.

"He's also a bit spoiled, in my opinion. Dogs belong outside, not inside."

"But it's not safe outside at night," I remind her.

"And that's exactly why the mutt is spoiled."

"You don't like dogs?"

Ruby shakes her head. "I've never really cared for any kind of canine. They're dirty, and you never know when one will turn on you. They're born predators. And from my experience, you can't tame a predator."

She reaches down and picks up my plate. "Sun is setting soon. Don't dawdle too long out here," she reminds me, then heads inside through the back door.

After a few more minutes of staring out at the prairie field, the sun getting closer to the horizon, I get up and walk over to the barn. I want to say good night to the horses. Inside the barn, two women wearing long skirts and aprons are locking the rear barn doors. When they come to the front ones, I meet them at the threshold.

"Can I stay with the horses for a bit?" I ask, not coming into the barn until they say it's all right.

The taller one nods. "Of course. Though, to get back to the inn, you'll have to go through the tunnels." She gestures toward an unlocked doorway on the side wall, which meets the neighboring structure. "The stairs are in there."

"Thank you," I say as I walk away. Talking to people without Bex is something I'm not used to. Before living with my sister, I'd go everywhere with our mother. All I've ever wanted is to be normal like everyone else, yet conversing with people and being around them, especially in large crowds, can be overwhelming. And the icy chill that spreads throughout my body whenever I get besieged by too many sounds and things to see, is definitely not something *normal* people feel.

I find Frostbite and Tumbleweed right where I left them after bringing them inside this afternoon from their time out in the corral. Before brushing them down, I freshen their hay pile and water trough. I brush Frostbite first, and when Tumbleweed nuzzles my arm, I know she's asking where Bex is.

"She'll be back tomorrow," I say, and give her muzzle a good rub. "Be patient." She's not and continues to push against my arm. "I'll get to you in a minute."

When it's time for me to start Tumbleweed, I pause at the chilling howl that pierces the silence from somewhere outside. No, not outside. I look to the ground covered in hay. When it happens again, both horses jerk. Their hooves dance in place at the sound. I try to settle them with calming commands, but the predator has them on alert. All of a sudden the stall feels too small, so I back out, closing the stall door.

"Oh, please settle, girls. Whatever it is, it's not in here." I hate seeing them all worked up like this. I sidestep to the next stall and to my surprise the horse in there is casually eating some hay. I move to the next stall. Same thing. This one's just standing there looking at me. No signs of distress or fear. I turn and face the horses on the other side. Same thing. Not a single one jittery or anxious.

"What in the hay is going on?"

Frostbite whinnies the second another howl cuts through the night. It has to be that wolf Maureen almost unleashed on us in the inn last night. And if it is, I'm betting she's got it chained up somewhere underground.

After saying goodnight to Frostbite and Tumbleweed, I walk to the room where the woman said the stairs were located. The inside is about the same size as the building Maureen showed us this morning next to the inn. Except this one is full of farming supplies, hanging on the wall and stockpiled on some sturdy wood shelves. The front window is covered by a large wood wall with a peep hatch, same as the other building.

Curious, I unlock the hatch and let it hang open on its hinges. Outside is dark, and the full moon casts a pale grayish-blue light over the town. Gravers Junction most definitely looks like a ghost town in this light.

The howl comes again, but this one ain't like the ones I've been hearing. It's less—powerful. My northern magic stirs, helping me decipher the threat. And when I hear a chorus of howls, I know those are coming from out there somewhere. This place is crawling with wolves. Inside and out. I'm about to close the hatch but hold it open when three wolves run into view. They head straight for the front doors of the inn, sniffing around before trotting out into the open street. They're not as big as the one Maureen has, but a wolf's a wolf—deadly and always on the hunt.

They howl in unison, and then stare out, each one watching a different building as if waiting for a response. When they don't get one, they run off out of sight.

I close the hatch and secure the lock. I see now why it's not safe to go outside at night. We had a wolf get into the chicken coop once. The aftermath was a gory sight to be seen. Thankful I don't have to go out there, I make my way underground to the secret tunnels. After closing the heavy wood door at the bottom of the stairwell, I stand in the hall, unsure of which direction to go. The tunnel, which is lined with floor to ceiling pine wood plank boards and lit by hanging lanterns extends out to my left and right. The townsfolk don't need signs telling them which way to go, but golly darn, I could use one or two right now.

Biting my lip and fiddling with the end of my braid, I stare down one direction, which is shrouded in darkness, and then the other. The obvious path is to follow the one that has the lanterns. But then a gust of air sweeps through the tunnel, rushing at me, whispering in my mind, *"Go. Go and see."*

Trusting the winds, I remove one of the lanterns from the wall and hold it out in front of me to light the way. Looking to the ceiling, I should be directly under the barn. Continuing through the dark, the floor sloping deeper underground, a shiver crosses my shoulders at the temperature drop. The pine boards lining the walls come to an end and the sides of the tunnel going forth are packed dirt with support beams every ten paces.

The tunnel continues, and I swear I must be out past the barn by now. Soft whimpers get louder, and when I finally reach a heavy wood door, I push it open and peek inside, holding the lantern in first.

A growl comes from the shadows at the far end of the room, followed by *clank*s of metal chains. Glowing yellow eyes find me and stare out as a massive form slowly emerges into the soft lantern light. It stalks forward, thick dark brown hair at attention along its hackles while it bares sharp white fangs.

"Easy, there," I say, my palm out to it. "I didn't mean to disturb you." I'm not actually sure what I'm doing in here. Why did I listen to the whispers? Then I stop and stand straight. The wolf also stops advancing, but it continues to growl. I take it as a warning not to come any closer. And I'm not sure if it stops because there's no more lead on its chains, or if it's assessing the intruder. I set the lantern down next to the doorway, and before sitting next to it, I close the door.

"I think the whispering winds wanted me to find you. I think they want us to get to know one another a little better." The ground is hard and cold, which oddly feels nice compared to the warm weather up on the main ground level. I silently wish there were a blanket or some hay to sit on, but this will have to do.

"Now, I believe Maureen mentioned your name was Hunter. And I'm going to assume that means you're a boy wolf, though my apologies if I'm wrong. My name is Nina, and I'm here with my sister, Bex. We're still deciding how long our stay in Gravers Junction will be, but regardless, this is a fascinating place. I'm quite impressed with this town and all the ways you all have adapted in order to survive."

While I speak, Hunter's growl softens until he isn't growling at all. I keep talking, and eventually he relaxes and lowers himself to the ground. He doesn't curl up or dip his head. He just sits there, keeping that yellow gaze on me.

After an hour, sleep beckons me. Standing, I brush the dust off my skirt. "I'd like to come back and visit you again tomorrow." The wolf tilts his head, not as if he doesn't understand me but as if he's asking, *You want to come back?*

"I'll bring two blankets, one for me and one for you. And maybe some snacks." I open the door and before slipping out, I say, "You shouldn't be left all alone down here in the dark." Then I set the lantern down and leave, closing the door behind me.

The whispering winds seem to want me to gain his trust, and that's what I plan on doing tomorrow. Sitting and talking with him, because he looks as if he could use a friend.

TEN

BEX

After supper, we clean up and make our way outside. The grit within my skin comes alive and ripples gently with awareness as we walk in a procession toward the rock formation. I've yet to understand its movements, and I hope the spirit we're about to summon will either remove the affliction or enlighten me with how to control it.

A beautiful full moon sits high in the clear, cloudless sky while white specks twinkle and dot the expansive darkness. Booker and Garrett lead the way, each holding rifles, while I follow close behind. Murphy takes up the rear, holding a short-barrel shotgun close to his chest.

If we were attacked right now, I wouldn't even know how to call upon my magic to help. This world of aberrants still feels unreal to me—like a story from a children's book. Yet here I am, with warm dust magic flowing through my body, following a werewolf to some sacred spot where we're going to call upon the Spirit of the Land. How does the world beyond the Graveyard Territory not know about all this?

I push the question out of my mind and stare past the men in front of me to the towering rock formation. Once we're there, Booker explains it's important to keep quiet and not to light any torches or fires.

While Garrett and Murphy talk quietly, Booker crouches next to a campfire site enclosed by smooth gray rocks. I get low next to him, the skirt of my dress bunching up around my knees, and whisper, "I thought you said no fires."

"I ain't making a fire." With one hand, he brushes off a layer of dirt from over the center of the pit. A giant flat stone with smooth edges sits perfectly in the middle of the stone circle. He picks up the oversized rock with such ease it reminds me of Ruby and her axe. Maybe Ruby's a werewolf too?

I stare at the dark hole he's revealed. "What's down there?"

He looks up at the sky and then to the hole. "You'll see." To Garrett, he quietly says, "We've got about twenty minutes before the moon is in place."

"What happens then?" I ask. I lean closer to the hole. Water drips from somewhere in the darkness.

"Murphy, you hang back here." Garrett sets his rifle against one of the giant boulders before coming over to me. "Come on," Garrett says, cupping his hand under my elbow and helping me to my feet. "It's dark, so stay close."

We follow Booker as he circles behind the rock formation while Murphy stays behind to guard the hole in the ground. I'm not sure where we're headed, but I don't ask. We're supposed to be quiet, for one thing, and for another, Garrett's hand distracts me, holding my arm and leading me through the dark.

Earlier, over supper, he argued with Booker about summoning the Spirit of the Land. Maybe he'd argue on anyone's behalf, not just mine. Regardless, it feels good, having someone care whether I get hurt.

Garrett leans close and whispers, "I sure hope you do not die tonight."

"And why is that?" I ask, honestly curious what my life means to him.

"Your sister would probably murder me if I come back without you."

I stop short, my boots sliding in the dirt, tugging his grip until he halts too. "What's wrong?" he asks, peering down at me in the pale moonlight.

"Are you interested in my sister?"

His hand drops from my arm. "Interested in what way?"

"I don't know. In a romantic way, I suppose." I've never been so bold about matters of the heart, especially with a man. And I find that I like it.

"Bex, let me be clear about something," he says. "I'm not looking for a wife."

"Yes, Maureen already made that clear," I cut in.

He ignores me. "My job is to keep people safe. To make sure they do not get killed by aberrants. Or malicious humans, since they're out here too."

His words settle in my stomach like a stone. So that's that. I mistook his kindness for something more, and now I know better.

"I will say," he adds, lifting a hand to brush a loose strand of hair from my face, "you are quite the woman."

My insides melt all the same, like butter on a hot day. I feel bolder than usual, but not bold enough to lean in for a kiss.

"Well, thank you," I say. "And you, Sheriff, are quite the man."

He steps closer. "No, you misunderstand—"

"You two coming, or not?" Booker whispers urgently from a distance.

"We should go," I say quickly, moving past Garrett. "We can talk later. If I survive the night."

It does not have to be him, I remind myself. But this moment has opened my eyes. Love may still be waiting for me somewhere.

We find Book standing at the base where two boulders touch, one narrower and resting against the other at an angle. In front is an overgrown shrub. Booker drags his boot along the ground until a hidden rope appears. He picks it up, loose dirt cascades off the twine, then walks backward, dragging the shrub away from the rock formation and revealing a hole large enough for a person to crawl through.

"The bush—it's not real," I say with enthusiasm. It's not everyday one is shown a secret cave entrance.

"No, ma'am, it's not." Booker drops the rope and comes over to where Garrett and I stand. "And I'd appreciate if you didn't tell anyone what you're witnessing tonight."

"You have my word," I promise. As I stare at the dark opening, fear grips my nerves. "How—how far do we have to crawl?" The idea of getting trapped in a small, tight space has me frozen where I stand.

Garrett whispers, "It's bigger than it looks, and doesn't go that far in before it opens up and you can stand. I promise you'll be fine." He lowers himself to the ground and then crawls into the dark space.

"You're next," Booker tells me, ushering me with a gentle push.

I hike up my skirt, giving my knees room to crawl. I'm wishing I wore my stockings underneath as sharp pebbles and rocks bite into the skin along my knees and legs, but it's so hot I didn't want to be uncomfortable sweating during our journey.

Garrett's right. The tunnel is short, and then his hand's there, helping me to stand. I take it, feeling his skin against mine. Not for the first time, since he took the liberty to grab my shoulders last night when he thought I was drowning in the tub or when he was holding my arm moments ago. This time, I have the chance to appreciate his touch—to feel the skin of his working hands. There are soft spots, and a few calloused ones.

"Thank you," I say, getting to my feet.

Booker is right behind me, and the second he stands, he moves to the left and fiddles with something metal. The soft clanking continues until a match strikes. A warm flame grows after he lights the wick inside the lantern, revealing a cozy, cavernous space.

"Follow me, and watch your step," Booker says, descending a narrow set of stone stairs spiraling beneath the ground.

That's what this rock formation must be for—to hide these stairs.

As we go deeper, the air and the stone walls become noticeably colder. At the bottom, there's another tunnel. The stretch of tunnel has a curved ceiling, carved high enough for Garrett and Booker to walk around without difficulty. I follow the glow of the lantern, and when we step out into the larger cavern, moonlight shines through the hole in the ceiling. It's not enough to reach the entire cavern, but Booker's lantern is ample light for us to see the space and the pool of water ahead. The water's surface is barely detectable from its stone surroundings.

"Why does the water look so murky?" I ask, moving closer.

"Careful," Booker warns. "It's deeper than it looks." Then he points up to the ceiling. Circling the pool of water are long rocks, tapered at the ends and looking more like icicles than rock. I swear there's an iridescent sheen to them. Water drips from the tips, and I follow its path. While some drops fall onto the water's surface, most land outside of the sunken pool, then slowly trickle down, adding to the water.

Booker looks to the ceiling of the cavern and whistles. Then, when a dark silhouette appears over the hole, he asks, "You good up there?"

Murphy's voice is low as he calls down to us. "Yeah! All quiet up here!"

"Stay alert!" Garrett adds before Murphy's form disappears from sight.

"All right, let's get you ready," Booker says, setting down the lantern. "See that?" He points to the pool of milky water. "The four elements of air, earth, water, and fire all meet in this sacred spot, and when combined with the direct path to the moon, well, that's the only time someone can call upon the Spirit of the Land."

"I don't see any fire?" I search the cavern, my gaze landing on the lantern. "Except for that."

"Yeah, that isn't the fire." Booker laughs. "You'll feel it in a minute."

A shiver zips along my shoulders, and I shudder at the cold air that sweeps in—from where, I have no clue. The lantern light helps illuminate this side of the cavern, but I don't know where the wall is on the other side.

"You okay?" Garrett asks, coming over to stand by the edge of the pool.

"Yeah. I just wish there was more light."

"You don't need more light," Booker says in a dismissive tone. "Now pay attention. You'll need to remove your clothing."

"My clothing?" I repeat his words with sharp emphasis.

"Yes, yes. Don't worry, nobody's going to be looking at you. The milky water will cover your parts up. You can't be wearing all those clothes if you want a direct connection with the elements."

"Is he lying?" I lean in and ask Garrett in a voice that's deliberately private.

"No, ma'am, he isn't lying." He rubs his knuckles over his short beard, along his jaw.

"I know it's harder for humans to be exposed," Booker says, dimming the lantern light. "It comes easier for us aberrants."

"I'm an aberrant now. And I don't think I'll ever get used to being naked in front of people," I mutter under my breath.

"You don't have to do this," Garrett says, turning my shoulders so I'm facing him. "You've been thrust into this world like a kid tossed into a lake who doesn't know how to swim. There will be other full moons. There's no rush. We can come back in a month, after you've learned more about the evils of this territory."

"Not all aberrants are evil, right?" I ask, holding his gaze.

He slides his hands from my shoulders, down my arms before dropping them to his sides. "No. But there's more evil than good out in these parts."

"I don't want to wait," I confess.

"If the Spirit of the Land will speak with you…and if she doesn't kill you…you should know that the connection is different for everyone. I don't know how it works for a dustslinger." He shifts his weight to the other hip before continuing, "What I'm saying is, unlocking the knowledge and power within you may also cause you pain…or it may be as simple as opening a door. I don't know."

I look over my shoulder to where Booker is. "What about you? Do you know what it'll be like if she speaks to me?"

The werewolf shakes his head. "Garrett's right. It's different for each of us."

"Great," I mutter. Then inhale a deep breath, and say to Garrett, "It'll be fine. I can handle it." Even if I'm not feeling it, I need to appear confident in order to get this done.

Booker leans out over the pool of water that's maybe the size of two copper tubs combined and stares up through the hole. "Yup, the moon is almost there." He takes his sunrider hat off and sets it on a nearby rock, lifts his leg, then grabs his boot and slides it off. "We'd best hurry and get in there."

I watch him in horror. He's getting in the water with me—and I'll be naked? Oh, hell no!

I back away, and Garrett looks between his friend and me, then says, "No. She's my charge, so I'll do it. I'll get in the water with her."

The two men hold their gaze for a heartbeat before Booker concedes. "Suit yourself." He slips his boot back on and picks up his hat. "I'll go up and keep watch with Murphy." Before leaving, he reminds me, "Nothing on your body. And when she comes, be honest with her. The Spirit of the Land always knows when someone's lying. Good luck to ya." Turning, he leaves us alone in the cavern.

I look to the hole and see the moon coming into view.

"Why does anyone have to come in with me?"

"In case something goes wrong. I can try to pull you back to the living."

"Wait, no one said anything about dying."

"You're not dying," he explains. "Your soul will be doing the conversing, that's all. And if the Spirit of the Land tries to kill you, well, then, that's why I'm here. To wake you from the trance."

"Now, I'll give you some privacy to undress. Holler at me when you're in the water." He leaves the lantern and disappears down the tunnel.

I take off my boots first, then unbutton the high collar of my dress. Before slipping it off, I shout, "You're not peeking, are you?"

"No!" His voice floats out from deep within the tunnel. He sounds as if he's pretty far back, so I hurry and remove my dress before folding it and setting it on a nearby rock.

Then, as I remove my undergarments, he shouts, "Are you in the water?"

"Not yet." With nothing on my body, I walk across the cold stone to the edge of the pool, and dip one foot in. It's surprisingly warm. Once I'm all the way in, the water gets hotter the deeper I sink in. This must be what Booker meant about fire. It doesn't burn. Rather, it's soothing against my tense muscles. I let a long sigh work its way free as my feet reach the bottom. Oh, I could get used to this. If I had one of these natural hot springs in my backyard, I'd probably be out here every night.

"Bex, we gotta hurry! Can I come out?"

"Oh, yes! Sorry!" I bend my knees a little so everything below my shoulders is covered by the milky water.

He emerges from the dark tunnel but stops short of seeing me. I turn around, giving him some privacy while he undresses. With my hair still pinned up, the cool air from the cavern grazes the tops of my shoulders. I lower myself deeper into the water until the surface grazes my chin.

A gentle lap of water pushes against my back as he gets in. "Oh, it's hotter than I remembered," he says, more to himself than to me.

"You'll keep your hands to yourself?" I ask.

"I'm a gentleman and would never put my hands on you…" There's a pause before he says in a playful tone, "Unless you asked me to."

I push my hand through the water and send a splash back at him. "Are you in? Can I turn around?"

"Yes, yes." He chuckles.

Slowly I face him. The water's surface hits below his

chest. I let my eyes take in the lines of his body, the muscles curving along his arms and shoulders. Then I lift my gaze to his, and we say nothing. What's there to say in this moment? I'm in a cavern, completely nude, submerged in a hidden underground hot spring with a stranger. His eyes stay focused on mine, except for the one or two times they dip. Heat blooms between my legs, and I know it's not from the hot spring.

Booker's voice echoes down to us from the hole above. "You two about ready?" Then, before we can answer, he chuckles as if seeing something funny we don't. "Listen, Bex," Booker says with all seriousness. "When the moon is in position, all you've got to do is close your eyes, think about the fire and water surrounding you, and the stone and air above you. Don't think about the sexy man in front of you—"

"Booker," Garrett scolds in a deep voice.

Booker laughs again. "Okay, sorry. Anyway, you get what I'm saying, Bex?"

"I understand," I call up to him. My knees straighten, making me taller, while also revealing the swell of my breasts. I only realize I've exposed more than I intended when Garrett's gaze breaks from my face, dipping lower than my lips, and he swallows hard. I quickly bend my knees again, lowering my body deeper into the water.

There's something there. He may not want to open his heart, but he's hungry for something. I can see it in the way he looks at me.

Stay focused. I squeeze my eyes shut and clear my mind. *Think about the elements. The warmth coming from deep underground, heating the water, along with the chill in the air as stone surrounds me from all sides.* I keep repeating the thought over and over, until I try and open my eyes—except I can't.

I flail my arms about, not caring if Garrett sees my bare skin.

Something's wrong.

The world around me disappears. I can't feel the warm water. Or the cool air. I stretch my toes, searching for the stone ground in the pool, but there's nothing. And then I realize there's no water. Nothing but air. I'm completely naked and floating through the air. I want to scream—to cover myself up and hide from whoever is looking at me. This is wrong. I shouldn't have done this. I feel exposed and vulnerable…and violated.

"Not violated." A voice speaks to me from the void behind my closed lids. *"Think of it as a test of your limits. Now, open your eyes, dustslinger, and make your case. If not, your soul is mine, and Malik Graves wins."*

ELEVEN

BEX

I open my eyes and relief floods my body, easing my panicked nerves. Everything's okay. Well, as okay as it can be while my body stands in the pool and my spirit form stands out in the cavern next to a woman wearing a high-collared dress. The bottom hem drags along the stone ground while her long sleeves go well past her hands. The entire garment is white with gold stitch detailing and short ruffles along the buttons down her chest. She looks like a wealthy woman from town, in the most plain but luxurious dress I've ever seen. Her silver hair is braided down her back, and her skin is flawless. She stares at me with such vibrance in her eyes, like a new friend just waiting to get to know everything about someone.

I look down at myself, now covered up with the dress I was wearing earlier, but more translucent. My entire body glows a soft white, and lifting my hand up, I can see the woman standing nearby straight through my flesh.

"Is this what being a ghost is like?" I ask.

"You are a curious creature," she says with a warm smile. "Persephone chose wisely. I can already see a spark of hope within you. But I know this world is not one you're familiar with. So, Rebecca Rose Ellington, I'll give you the opportunity to make your case. Whatever I decide, is what will be."

"Make my case?" I repeat her words, unsure of her exact meaning. Which case am I to present? Remove the dustslinger powers, tell me how to master those powers, or take me to where Levi is so I can live out my eternal afterlife with him? What case am I to make when I know nothing about this supernatural world? Maybe I should've listened to Garrett and waited before calling on the Spirit of the Land.

"Well, dear. I *have* all night, but you—you're running out of time."

"What does that mean?"

A howl sounds from outside the hole. I look up to see wolves leaping over the hole. The sounds of growls mix with those of jaws snapping.

"Oh, I have to help! Garrett needs to help them!" I startle and quickly face the Spirit of the Land. "Can I come back another time?"

She shakes her head. "And how do you plan on helping them?"

"What?" My frantic gaze shifts from the hole to her. "I know how to shoot. I'll do whatever I can to help."

She moves closer and I stare into her eyes. They possess every color, gently swirling like tight rainbows deep, deep inside her eyes. It's like looking across the prairie land and seeing the sunset balled up and spinning round and round.

"Why not use what's inside you to fight them?"

With a flustered shrug, I tell her, "I would if I knew how! And I don't think we have time for you to teach me, not with Booker and Murphy in trouble."

She waves a hand, and the sounds of fighting and teeth snapping vanish. "It hasn't come to be—yet."

I tilt an ear to the sky, listening. All is quiet. "You mean that fight hasn't happened yet?"

The spirit nods. "We've got some time to talk." She lowers herself onto a smooth stone bench and pats the space next to her.

I move to her side. "Listen, you're right. This is all new to me. And I don't know if I want to live in this dangerous world. But right now, I need to understand exactly what a dustslinger is and if it's possible to remove it."

"Is that what you want? To rid yourself of this power? If so, make your case and it shall be done. If that's not the case you wish to make, then choose wisely. You only get one chance, and then I decide your fate."

"No," I say, jumping to my feet and standing before her.

"No?" This time it's her repeating my words as if no one has ever told her no.

"That's right, you heard me. You don't get to decide my fate. And I sure as hell am not making my case without knowing all the information there is to know."

She stands, except her form grows taller, towering over me and arching as though she's about to swallow me whole. "You dare to speak to the Spirit of the Land in such a disrespectful tone." Her voice booms throughout the cavern, and I swear I see Garrett's body tremble in the water.

The spirit raises a hand, palm facing me. There's a pain in my head and behind my chest that throbs, as if my soul is being ripped out of me. My feet lift off the ground and I float before her. The pain grows more intense, and I fear the Spirit of the Land has had enough time to decide my fate.

This is it. This is my end. I float higher into the cavern, as my physical body starts to convulse in the pool. Garrett immediately lunges forward and grabs my shoulders. He's shouting something, but I can't hear him. He raises a hand as if he's going to slap me but stops. Instead, he brings his mouth to mine.

The act causes the Spirit of the Land to shrink and gush like a youthful girl excited for her friend at such an intimate gesture. She kneels by the side of the pool and whispers, "Oh, what an interesting turn of events!"

The threat of losing my soul to this mystical being fades, and my spirit form slowly descends until my feet reach the ground.

Not paying any attention to me, she spreads her hands wide as if to embrace Garrett, but doesn't. Tears stream her cheeks as she professes, "The benefactor's heart beats again."

Garrett pulls back, breathless, as my convulsions settle. He waits, his hands still gripping my shoulders tightly. I can't even imagine the anticipation he must be experiencing—will she wake up and live, or will the spirit claim her and die.

The spirit looks up at me, and her annoyed expression melts into a compassionate one. She stands, comes over to me, and cups my face with her hands. "I see it now. I see your destiny. You are not the one to save Gravers Junction, no, my dear. But you are a protector, and you'll need to be strong in order to play your part."

"Thank you," I say, unsure of her meaning. "Does that mean I may live, and you'll help me understand how to use my dustslinger powers?"

"If that's what you want."

I nod. The decision was easier than I'd thought it would be. I don't want her to take it from me.

"I grant you knowledge and a tether to the Spirit of the Land," she whispers before leaning in and kissing my forehead.

A rush of wind comes at me, throwing my spirit body through the air. There's something pressing into my skull, and I scream as the pressure passes through bone and into my mind. Time seems to slow, and my eyes are overcome by the brightest light. A heavy weight inside my mind lifts, and I'm struck with a sense of familiarity. The sand stirs beneath my skin, and I know exactly what it's telling me: *Get ready, we're about to fight.*

Something inside my muscles unlocks as well, and I'm seeing myself sparring with a werewolf, not in beast form but looking like a human, dodging punches and moving with accuracy I didn't know I could do.

"I will see you again," the Spirit of the Land whispers in my mind.

When I open my eyes, I get my wish. Garrett's hands are gripping my shoulders, and his gaze is intensely focused on my face. When I blink, his hands instantly go to my face. "Bex?"

"Still alive," I say with a small chuckle.

He pulls me in for a giant hug, his arms wrapping around my naked body. I don't move my own, a bit shocked at the gesture. When he realizes I haven't returned the gesture, he quickly releases me and moves back, the water splashing and rippling between us.

"My apologies. I'm just grateful you're okay."

Another chuckle escapes, and his panicked reaction simmers with the sound. He offers me a small smile. "I truly am sorry to have intruded on your space."

"You saved me," I say. "The Spirit of the Land was about to claim my soul, and then stopped when you kissed me."

"You saw that?"

"Like I said, you saved me."

"I needed to wake you, but I didn't want to hurt you."

"The spirit saw something in that moment. She also called you 'the benefactor.' You want to tell me what that means?"

He shakes his head and instead of answering, he asks, "So? What happened?"

"She unlocked it all," I say while pressing the tips of my fingers to my head. "I know exactly how to use the dustslinging powers now."

He lets out a massive sigh. "Oh, thank the gods."

I nod, then climb out of the water, not caring if he sees me naked—again. When I glance over my shoulder, curious to know if he's watching me, to my delight, he is. And I swear, as I grab my dress and disappear down the tunnel, I hear a soft groan from that man's lips.

"Come on! Hurry and get dressed! There are wolves coming, and we need to be ready!"

TWELVE

BEX

It takes me longer than expected to get my dress on with my skin damp from the water. Garrett is done before me, and when he comes down the tunnel, I'm putting on my boots.

"The spirit showed you an attack?"

I nod. "I thought it was happening in real time, but she said no—it was to come."

"You stay here, and I'll go tell Booker and Murphy. No one will find you here if I push the shrub over the cave entrance."

"Don't you dare!" I snap, leaving the laces of my boots untied and finish fastening the last few buttons along the high collar of my dress. "I'm coming with you!"

"Like hell you are!" he says, stepping closer as if his towering height would intimidate me.

Maybe before my encounter with the Spirit of the Land, but now that everything is unlocked…oh, hell no. I feel like a new woman.

I push past him. "Please. I can have you on your ass lying on the ground in a heartbeat." Or at least I think I can. I've yet to test my newfound strength, which makes me even more anxious to get to the surface. Then I feel the dust shifting behind my chest, and somehow I know exactly what it's preparing to do.

Oh, this is going to be fun.

"And besides," I say with a smirk before the power works its magic, "I'm already gone." Then, as if my mind is holding a rope to my destination, I pull hard at the invisible tether anchored at the spot where I want to go. My body turns to a giant dust cloud, and I feel weightless. I can still see the world around me, enjoying Garrett's startled expression and him almost tripping over his own feet, as I travel faster than the wind up to the surface. Releasing the tether, my body reappears outside. My feet stagger about a bit before turning and racing out from behind the rock formation.

Booker and Murphy are there, firearms in hand, searching their surroundings. The moon casts a pale light, though it's still hard to see movement out in the prairie. Booker's hound dogs are barking from the cabin in the distance.

"Wolves," I say. "The Spirit of the Land showed me we'd be attacked by wolves."

"Not wolves," Booker clarifies. "Werewolves."

Oh. Shit.

"The spirit showed me the attack, except they were wolves not in human form," I tell Booker.

"Yeah, well, the Spirit of the Land sees those before her as their aberrant lineage. So a werewolf, in their human or wolf body, would be seen as a wolf."

"Huh, that's interesting."

Movement through the tall grass out somewhere in the dark has all three of us looking in the same direction. I can do this. The knowledge is there. My body knows how to fight. I just need to embrace everything and be confident.

"What happens if I get bitten?" I ask under my breath, searching the darkness.

"Don't," he says, then stands erect, on alert. His head cocks slightly as if he hears something.

"What is it?" Murphy asks, short-barrel shotgun ready in his arms.

"It's just me," Garrett grumbles, coming around from behind the rock formation with the lantern in one hand. He grabs the rifle and gets in line with the rest of us.

"The you-know-what back in its place?" Booker asks.

"Yeah, and I covered the rope with dirt." He sets the lantern down, and the glow makes it harder to see movement in the distance. Turning it off is also not an option as once the fighting begins, we'll need ample lighting.

"Good. Don't need these pieces of shit knowing where that healing pool is."

The water is also a place to *heal*? I pocket that piece of information for when I need it. If I'm going to be living out in this forsaken territory, I imagine there may come a time when we'll need some magic healing water.

A howl breaks the silence.

"They're coming," Booker says. To me, he offers a pistol from his holster around his waist.

I wave a hand at him. "I don't like guns. Besides, I know what I'm doing now." With concentrated thought, I imagine a dust cloud forming in my palm, and one does. It's beautiful. As though I'm holding a miniature storm in my hand. When I close my fist, the storm dissipates, sand cascading through my fingers.

The sorrow that reflects in his eyes confuses me, but then I recall that he and Persephone were lovers. I'm the new dustslinger, yes, but I'll never replace what she meant to him or the people she protected. I'll have to be something else to them.

"You good?" I ask, and he nods, shaking off the moment.

His arm goes out straight in front of me and pushes me back. I stumble, almost tripping over the bottom of my dress just as a slender form lunges out from the darkness, straight for me. The creature tumbles into a somersault, then bounces up with a spin before landing on its feet facing us. "Hello, Booker. It's been a while since we've seen you at the pack meetings. Oh wait, you've been banned from the pack meetings." Her cackle is high-pitched and quite annoying.

Two more werewolves creep their way out of the shadows and into the small circle of lantern light. "Lookie here," the broader of the men says. His hair is long and scruffy, with a dark beard to match. "Did you bring your food out to play?"

"You gonna share?" the other asks. This one is shorter than I am, but just as hairy as the broad werewolf guy. Both have tufts of hair trailing down the bridge of their nose.

Behind them three giant wolves pace. Aside from their lighter underbellies, their fur is dark. Their glowing yellow eyes are focused on us.

"You aren't welcome on my plot, and as an alpha, you can either bow to me or get the fuck off my land!" Booker heaves in shallow breaths as he seethes. "Leave now!"

The shorter wereman tsks then shifts his mouth into a wicked smile. "Nice try, old man. We know pack law. Anyone who pledges loyalty to a banned alpha gets put on the kill list."

"I don't want to be your fucking alpha," Booker says between gritted teeth.

"No," the werewoman chimes in, her long, dark, unkempt hair clearly in need of a good wash and brush. "But the second we follow one of your *orders* it could be mistaken as an act of loyalty." Dry dirt smears her forehead and cheeks, and she has a patch of hair trailing the bridge of her nose, like her two male companions, except it's not as thick as theirs.

The taller wereman takes a step closer. My gaze dips, I swear his fingernail-claws are extending even longer.

"We have a message for you," the werewoman says, stalking over. I sidestep out of the way, letting her approach Booker without interference. "Cletus wants to remind you of your place."

I'm not sure what their meaning is. How are they going to remind him of his place? Then Garrett shouts, "It's against pack law to attack another alpha! Regardless of his banned status!" The intruders don't acknowledge his presence. The wolves circling us in the tall grass move closer to Garrett.

"You do this, and I have the right to bring it to the council," Booker says with a low growl.

"Go for it, old man," the short one taunts.

"We can take 'em," Murphy says, cocking the rifle.

"No, you can't," Booker warns in a threatening tone. "Do not engage. Back away and let me handle this. Getting involved only makes things worse for everyone."

The sheriff whistles while holding an arm out, waving to step back, and Murphy obliges. Garrett gestures for me to follow, but something inside of me snaps. I'll not stand by and watch Booker be attacked.

"I'm with Murphy. Let's dance," I say, excited for my first fight—my chance to see what this unlocked knowledge and power can do. Like before, my body pulls on that invisible rope, and I disappear in a burst of dust before reappearing right next to the shorter man. He snarls at me, razor-like nails extending out from the tips of his fingers.

"Dustslinger!" he shrieks, then releases a howl up into the night sky. The wolves around us also start howling.

I slam my foot into his side, which causes his howl to become a painful whimper. Garrett and Booker shout my name, while the other two werewolves move shoulder to shoulder, deep growls reverberating up from their throats.

A loud *boom* ignites, and I turn to see smoke slipping out of the end of the shotgun barrel. I follow its path and see the woman holding a clawed hand over her shoulder, blood seeping out from behind it.

"You'll pay for that, you thievin' rustler," she seethes.

Meanwhile, I let the sand from my arm collect with more sand from the ground and form a long rope. I whip it out and the end wraps around the shorter man, tying his arms to his sides. My thoughts command the rope to squeeze, and it does, grains of sand trickling free from the sandrope.

Another shot echoes through the air, and the man I've secured flies back, the sandrope exploding from the bullet. The man doesn't get up. Blood stains the red dirt beneath his lifeless body.

Seeing his body lying there startles something inside me. I stare at the man who will never take another breath, never speak another word, and never see another day. That's how fast everything can end. Is that how fast Levi's last moments went down?

The wolves growl and snap their jaws, but they don't advance. Distracted by their presence, I'm caught off guard when someone slams into me. I'm thrown hard onto the ground. The pain from the abrupt fall has me struggling to replace the air forced from my lungs. The wereman rolls onto his side and claws at the earth, trying to grab me. Amidst trying to escape, I find the strength to breathe again. He eventually gets hold of my ankle and drags me closer until I'm pinned beneath him.

"Get off of me!" I scream. His face is inches from mine, breathing heavy, hot breaths onto my face.

The dust within me is frantic, rattling my bones as if it had a voice and were screaming for me to move. But I can't. Instead, I turn my head to the side, not wanting to look death in the face.

"Bex!" Garrett shouts, and I open my eyes to see him running toward us, the barrel of his weapon aimed at the aberrant on top of me. "Vanish! Do that disappearing thing—now!"

Working through my fears, I do as he says and I reach for that invisible tether. My body *poofs* into a giant dust cloud as I transport myself from under my assailant to over where Booker and Murphy stand.

The wereman abruptly gets up and is immediately met with the end of Garrett's rifle. "Consider your next move carefully," Garrett warns.

The aberrant bares his sharp canine teeth, growling at Garrett. But the werewoman, still holding a hand to the hole in her injured shoulder, tugs at his arm. "Let Cletus deal with them. You know what happens when you face off with a dustslinger."

He growls again, but then his expression slackens, and he smiles. "You started this, Sheriff. Not us. You."

"We didn't start shit!" I say, cursing out loud for the first time too. It feels liberating. "You came here looking for trouble!"

The broad-shouldered one hoists the fallen werewolf over his shoulder before he and the werewoman run off, the wolves trailing behind. Before they get too far, the woman shouts, "We'll be seeing you!" with a cackle in her voice.

Once they're gone, Booker looks at me with disappointment. "The Spirit of the Land might have given you knowledge about your powers and abilities, but she sure as hell didn't give you the rule book about Graveyard Territory."

"What?" I exclaim, following the three men back to Booker's home. "They were going to kill you! I had to do something!"

Garrett turns to me. "Maybe. But it's not our place to get involved. The moment you do, their fight becomes our fight."

"And?" I ask. "We could've taken them," I say with a rejuvenated sense of strength.

He shakes his head. "No, not our fight." He points to me and the two men making their way into Booker's home. "Everyone in our clan. And our clan isn't just us three. You just brought the fight to the people of Gravers Junction."

Well, damn. I guess there's still a lot to learn about the aberrant world and its rules.

THIRTEEN

NINA

Ruby is the only one to see me before I sneak off to bring Hunter some breakfast. She doesn't question me as I pile twice as much food, some coffee, and few large jars of water onto a tray. She asks if she can help, but I don't want her knowing where I'm going.

I like Ruby because she's the one I relate to most. She's cheerful, attentive, and genuinely kind, with a love for cooking and gardening. In many ways, she's the kind of *normal* I aspire to be.

The sun's been up for at least an hour by the time I get to the barn. Luckily, I don't cross paths with any of the townsfolk. After saying good morning to Frostbite and Tumbleweed and refilling their hay and water, I take my tray full of provisions underground, straight to Hunter's room.

The second I unhook the latch, defensive growls fill the air. "It's only me," I say, easing my way through the door with the oversized tray. The jars of water wobble, clanking against each other as I hasten to set the tray on the packed dirt. The growling stops, and while shutting the door, I look over at him. He's low to the ground, head up, watching me with those yellow eyes. Beneath his front legs is the blanket I brought over earlier this morning. Unsure of how much lead the chains allowed, I tossed the blanket over to him from the door where I knew he couldn't reach.

"Good wolf," I say, closing the door behind me. I set up a picnic across the room with my food and coffee and then offer some of the bacon to him. I approach him slowly, holding out the three strips of bacon in one hand. His yellow eyes remain locked on my face rather than the warm meat. When he shows his teeth, I know that's close enough.

"Here you go." I toss him the bacon just as I did with the blanket, which he must appreciate because he's sitting on top of it. Not sure about the bacon though. He doesn't give the meat any consideration, keeping his attention fixed to the stranger closing in on his personal space.

I return to my picnic blanket to eat my breakfast and drink my coffee, and eventually Hunter sniffs the bacon thrown at his paws and eats. When my stomach is full, I pick up the book I'd brought down earlier with the blankets and hold it in my lap. The tray sits close by, with enough food and water to last through lunch, knowing I'd want to spend the day down here earning the wolf's trust.

Before I start reading to Hunter, I feel the urge to tell him a little about myself.

"Being social and overly curious has always been more Bex's way. I tend to avoid people. Part of it is not wanting to be seen as different, and part of it is the habit of keeping my guard up. I never had trouble using Levi's old rifle on the farm, but put me in a room full of people and I panic.

"It's different here. I don't feel that anxiety as much when I'm with Maureen, Ruby, or even Garrett. There's something about this place that feels right. Like I don't have to pretend to be someone I'm not, even if I don't yet know who I'm meant to be.

"So I take it one day at a time. Maybe that has something to do with my northern heritage. I barely remember that life after running away so young. All I have now from that part of my life is my connection to the whispering winds. The voices that sweep into my thoughts, riding the wind like a wild stallion. I don't know who they are or why I can hear them, but their voices have been with me for so long I can't imagine a life without them."

Hunter's head rests on his two front paws. His eyes are closed. I like to think he enjoys my company, so I keep my efforts going and read from the book to him.

Some time later, after finishing up the chapter, I quietly close the book, trying not to wake the sleeping wolf. He's so beautiful with that thick coat blending in different shades of dark brown and a hint of white trailing his underside. His paws are almost as big as my breakfast plate. And strangely, for being locked up in an underground room, he doesn't smell awful. There's a faint pine tree scent mixed with fresh soil. He smells like an enchanted forest—if ever one exists. Fresh morning dew on the leaves of a thick forest, fog rolling along the ground, while morning sunlight breaks through the treetops, illuminating the forest in a magical atmosphere.

That's what I picture when I try to place his scent.

I lay my head on the extra blanket I brought and close my eyes, allowing myself to drift off to sleep. My thoughts explore what it might be like to find such a magical forest.

A gentle wind caresses my face, sweeping me away into a dream.

I'm walking between giant trees, the bark dark with rough detailing. Hunter comes up from behind, the top of his head grazing my fingers. He steps ahead of me, letting my fingers trail down his back through his thick, soft fur. The wind rushes at us as the day instantly turns to night. A full moon lingers through a break in the treetops. I've never seen the moon so close before, and it keeps growing in the sky as if coming straight for us.

Strong fingers lace through mine, and I look to see a tall man standing beside me. His brown hair is familiar, wild as it blends in with his short beard. Bushy eyebrows hood his glowing yellow eyes while a thin tuft of dark hair trails the bridge of his nose.

"Hunter?" I ask, already knowing in my heart it's him.

He smiles down at me and says, "Thank you, Nina."

"For what?"

"For treating me with kindness, and not like a monster."

"I don't believe in monsters."

He turns fully toward me, and I face him in return.

"I will protect you," he says, cupping my face in his hand. His claws rest against my cheek, careful, almost reverent. "Because monsters are real."

"And I will protect you," I whisper, smiling as the truth settles. He doesn't frighten me. He's in there, inside the wolf sleeping not ten feet away. "I *will* find a way to free you."

"Nina," he says my name softly, but there's a warning in it. "The wolf you see out there… it's me, but also not me. I've been cursed to live my days as a feral beast. When I wake, the memory of who I am fades like a dream I can't hold onto."

His condition breaks my heart. Tears burn behind my eyes.

"The human part of me is still here," he continues, his thumb gently wiping away a tear that's escaped. "But it's buried. Imprisoned deep within my mind by a spell I cannot break. Every morning, I lose myself again. And I don't know if there will ever be a day I wake and remember you."

"I won't give up on you." I take his other hand and press it over my heart. "What is it you need, or want?"

His hand flexes against me. "I cannot have what I want right now. But I will do everything I can to find a way out. You've given me a new purpose. A reason to live."

The wind swirls around us, rising and falling until our heartbeats move in sync. "I believe you won't forget me when you wake."

He glances at the air as leaves and small flowers lift around us. "Are you doing that?"

I nod. "It's time I embrace who I truly am and use whatever power I have to help free you."

We lie together in the heart of the forest, holding one another. I don't know what it means that Hunter exists as a man within my dreams, only that I want to stay here with him, where he can protect me from the monsters.

FOURTEEN

BEX

Booker decides to return to Gravers Junction with us. We help him fortify his home, locking his two hound dogs inside to protect his belongings. Booker insists they'll be safe, and that they're not completely cooped up. They have a way to get inside the barn, and then from there there's a small door that leads to a caged outdoor pen.

After saying goodbye to his furry companions, he tosses his saddle up on the roof of the stagecoach, ties his horse to the back, and sits with me inside the cabin. It's nice to have company rather than sit here in silence for four hours.

A few hours into our trek home, I've learned more about the laws of this land. Besides werewolf packs, there are also vampire clans, bug people, and a small group of demons that have taken residence in a mountain range on the far west side of Graveyard Territory. Booker explains that mostly, each kind keeps to its own land, but occasionally there are the drifters that enjoy stirring up trouble.

I have so many questions. I don't even know where to begin. After my encounter with the Spirit of the Land, a newfound confidence was unlocked alongside the knowledge of how to call upon the dustslinger powers and physical strength. I recall how easy it was to get out of the hot spring knowing Garrett was there, watching me. That was something I wouldn't have considered ever doing until the Spirit of the Land empowered me with this level of confidence. I feel like a whole new woman, and I can't wait to tell Nina all about it!

Booker continues to share his experiences and lessons about life in Graveyard Territory, and with each story, I'm both wary and thrilled to explore all of it. There's so much to know, not just about the beings that live here, but about the rules of engagement.

He's just finished telling me about an encounter with an entomonian. One of them had strayed too far from its home in the canyons down in the southwest region of the Graveyard Territory.

"So, have you ever visited these bug people?"

He smiles and shakes his head. "They're not really the welcoming kind. Skittish and all. Out of all the aberrants out here, they're the ones you'll encounter the least. They're harmless, mostly annoying." He drags his hand over his dark beard. "They have no sense of humor. Everything is strategic and with a purpose. They sleep, eat, mate, and go about their underground city lives. Honestly, I have no idea what they do. I do know they hate cold weather, so that's why they keep to the south."

I would never force Nina to stay, not in a place with such dangers, but I think I might want to stay. I also don't want to let go of my farm. There's a lot my sister and I need to talk about.

"You know, I can't recall the last time I saw Persephone in a dress," Booker points out, nodding toward my dress. The bottom hem is soiled up to my knees from being wet and dragging along the cave floor while I slipped it back on. The top and sleeves are smeared here and there with red dirt from the fight with the werewolves. I can't even imagine what my hair must look like. I'm looking forward to soaking in the copper tub.

"Where you from again?" Booker asks, tapping two fingers lightly on one knee.

"From Billingsworth County."

"Oh, that's right. I think you did mention that. Are you familiar with Seymour Heights?"

I was familiar with it. Levi sometimes picked up extra work there. It was one of the larger towns in Billingsworth, not the closest one where Nina and I usually went for our weekly supplies. On special occasions, though, we would travel there just to window-shop and admire the hustle and bustle. The sidewalks were always crowded, and the streets alive with horse-drawn carriages and riders. Levi once promised that one day he'd earn enough to spoil me with more than just a copper tub. He took that promise, and that life, with him into the afterlife.

"I am familiar with it."

"Have you crossed paths with a man named Ambrose Redding. He's a banker—or works closely with the banks."

The name tastes sour on my tongue. Lifting my chin high, trying to act as if the name doesn't make me want to curse, I say, "I am also familiar with Mr. Redding. He arranged the loan for my husband to build our home and farm."

Brows pinching, he tilts his head and asks, "You're married?" Then, looking over his shoulder, toward the front of the carriage, he laughs and shakes his head. I know he's wondering about the connection between me and Garrett. He sighs, composing his amusement, and says, "I assumed you were unmarried."

"Well, that would be an accurate assumption, because I *was* married. My husband was killed four years ago."

Booker leans back in his seat. "My condolences. Seems fate knew you were due for a fresh adventure."

I offer him a small smile, because yes, he's right, but also a part of me longs to return to that simple life. "It does seem that way."

"I think you'll do just fine"—he points to my hands—"with dustslinging. Plus, the people of Gravers Junction are the best people you'll ever meet. They know how to take care of each other—treat everyone in town like family."

"What about those who don't live in town?" Generally, I keep my inquisitive thoughts to myself, but this newfound confidence encourages me to speak more openly. "Like you."

A half-smile curves at one corner of his mouth. "There are those of us who share a mutual understanding with Maureen, like me. Sometimes, it's the laws of the land that supersede the honors of friendship, and Maureen knows this.

Without rules, this place would fall into darkness. No one would be safe from anyone." He pauses, then adds, "The elders, the council, whatever they're called in a given region, oversee their territory and keep their kind in check.

"I have no family or loyalty to anyone but me. I'm a drifter. Though, some sound advice—friend or foe, it's good to keep company with all kinds of people out here. You'll learn that well enough."

I pocket that information for another day. And as of today, I consider Booker a friend more than a foe. There are so many secrets about this territory and its people. "Tell me more about the people of Gravers Junction. Why do they live out here with all this danger lurking about?"

He inhales a deep breath and slowly lets it out while glancing out the open window. The flat plains haven't changed since we departed his plot. Nothing but open sky and tall grass. "I think that's a question for Maureen. I'm happy to talk about the monsters and the laws of the land, but the inner workings and the reasons behind Gravers Junction—well, that's not my story to tell."

"Fair enough," I say. "How about you tell me about vampires?"

He slides his tongue along his teeth, then sucks sharply before answering me. "I'd avoid those bloodsuckers if I were you. Even with your dustslinging powers, which I have to say that disappearing act you pulled last night on those wolves was impressive. Persephone couldn't do anything like that. Even so, the red-fang monsters are the worst of the worst. I'd rather duke it out with a half-breed demon than face one of them slippery suckers."

"Geez, you make them sound like there's no winning," I say, folding my hands gently in my lap. "Persephone must've fought one or two in her time?"

"Oh, she did. And barely came out alive. Santana is the worst, and he knows it. Stay clear of that motherfucker and you'll be just fine." He nods to the old leather satchel he gave me with Persephone's journal inside. "All her stories are in there. You'll want to read and memorize every word she wrote."

I rest a hand atop the bag and think about how I should keep a journal with my stories, in case one day I'm gone and the next dustslinger needs references.

"You know I can't quite place your age. You say you were married, yet you look awfully young."

Another smile, appreciating his compliment. "I'm twenty-seven. Born on the autumn equinox."

"I'll have to remember your birthday come fall."

"Oh, we rarely celebrate birthdays." My attention drifts from him to out the window. The sun is getting close to the straight line of the horizon. I imagine Garret will make sure we're back in Gravers Junction before dark. But staring out at the sunset reminds me of my parents' tradition of how we celebrated our birthdays. "There is one tradition my family always did when I was a child whenever someone's birthday rolled around."

"What's that?" Booker asks.

"We'd go on a picnic. A day of laughing and talking, spending time with one another, leading up to lying under the stars." I miss those picnics. Distracted by the heartfelt memories, I rub my hand against the stagecoach door. The wood is worn, showing age in spots where the dark stain has rubbed off. Lifting my chin, I inhale a calming breath and say, "You know, I think I might revive our traditional birthday picnics."

"Sounds good to me. Tell me when, and I'll be there." He adjusts his posture, stretching his arms before picking up his hat and setting it on his head. From beneath, his shaggy dark locks curl and stick out unevenly. "I guess we'll take it day by day for now, and see how you feel, being on a new adventure and all, come autumn."

"I guess we will," I counter with a smile. "You'll like my sister. She's a year older than me and sees the good in everyone."

"That'll change quickly if you two decide to stick around. Trusting the wrong individual out here will get a person killed. And not just killed, but depending on who's doing the killing, it could be a slow, torturous death."

My mouth purses in tense realization. "I'll make sure she understands that and keeps a better guard up."

"I reckon that's a good idea," he agrees.

"Gravers Junction up ahead!" Murphy calls from the driver's bench where he and Garrett sit.

"Oh, man. I hope Ruby has some of that frozen cream made. Man, that stuff is delicious."

I laugh at how right he is. There's a lot I'm starting to like about Gravers Junction. I stare up at the front of the stagecoach, where a certain someone sits up on the driver's bench beside Murphy.

FIFTEEN

BEX

While Booker and I make our way over to the inn, Garrett privately converses with Maureen. Her amiable facial expression drops, becoming serious and somewhat gloomy, as if the news of my mistake has cast a shadow over her mood. She looks to the entrance of town, out to the horizon where the sun disappears below the earth.

Garrett leaves her to her thoughts and helps Murphy walk the horses towing the stagecoach to the barn.

It's been a long time since I've been reprimanded like a child, and as Maureen walks our way, I feel it coming. What Maureen doesn't know is that, mistake or not, I won't be berated for something she could've prevented by telling us exactly what we were dealing with when we first arrived. It would've been helpful to know about the aberrants and the related rules of conduct, considering that she had multiple occasions to share this information, specifically at supper on the first night, during the tour that took place yesterday morning, and also before I left to go visit a werewolf out in Graveyard Territory. There's no way she's getting up in my face and blaming me for this.

"Well, you sure have put us in a bad situation." She crosses her arms and shakes her head at me.

"Yeah, well, maybe if I had known beforehand werewolves existed and there are laws that need to be followed, we wouldn't be in this situation." I mirror her stance and cross my arms over my chest, shooting her a pointed glare. I don't miss the look of surprise in her eyes, as if no one has ever challenged her authority.

Dropping her arms and moving past me, she says to Booker, "I imagine Cletus will be here soon." She looks over her shoulder at the setting sun.

He nods, rubbing his forehead under the brim of his sunrider hat. "I imagine he will, especially knowing there's a new dustslinger in town."

She exhales a heavy sigh and rubs under her nose. "Dammit, Book. If he finds Hun—"

"He won't," Booker cuts her off. "That's why I'm here."

Maureen nods. Then, as she walks by to head inside the inn, she cups his shoulder and says, "I appreciate that, more than you'll ever know. Now, come on, Ruby's got some of your favorite stew for dinner."

"Yes, ma'am. Right behind you." He gives me a wink before rushing off to get some supper.

I'm going to have to make it clear to Maureen that if I stay, no more secrets. Not just in teaching me the formalities of the land, but whatever secrets people have here—they all need to be laid out on the table. If I'm to be their protector, then I need to know everything about this place and its residents.

My stomach grumbles, and I follow the others into the inn, hoping Nina's inside helping Ruby. Though I'm disappointed that she didn't come out to welcome me back.

Inside, I hurry upstairs to our room only to find it's empty. Huh, where is she? Before heading downstairs, I quickly change out of my filthy dress and into a clean one. I'd love to fill the copper tub with hot water and soak for a bit, but finding my sister and eating some supper come first.

As I descend the stairs into the main parlor, Garrett and Murphy are there. While Murphy locks the front doors, Garrett walks over and meets me at the stairs. "It's nothing to worry about, really. Maureen will handle Cletus."

"You shot and killed one of them," I remind him.

"And that wouldn't have happened if you'd listened to me."

"Will they attack?"

Garrett shrugs one shoulder. "Let's hope Cletus is more interested in meeting the new dustslinger, because around here blood shed means blood is owed."

I already hate this Cletus fellow.

"I'll do better," I say. "I'll learn the laws and do better next time."

"Next time?" he asks, repeating my words. "Does that mean you've decided to stay?"

I want to tell him yes, but something in my gut says I need more time to think on the matter. "Let's focus on getting through tonight. Then maybe we can talk about permanent situations."

"Listen," he says, shuffling closer to the stair wall and resting his sunrider hat on top of the piano. "Whatever happens tonight, stay close to me. I know you've got your dustslinger powers, but until you can anticipate the threat before you, your powers aren't going to help you."

I recall how that massive wereman pinned me to the ground last night. "All right." Though, Cletus, this alpha werewolf, is coming here to meet the new dustslinger, which is me. That means I'm going to be involved one way or another. And hiding behind Garrett isn't a good look for the new dustslinger. But I don't argue with Garrett. I just nod and let him think he's in control.

Honestly, I don't know who has the upper hand in the upcoming squabble. Cletus or us. Maureen sure is frightened about Cletus being here and finding something she doesn't want him to find. And Booker knows what it is. Dammit. This town has too many secrets.

Garrett scrubs one hand through his wavy brown hair. "Cletus may be an outlaw, but he's always played by the werewolf rules. Plus," he says, with an optimistic tone, "we've got Booker here to testify about what actually happened last night. Who knows what story those mangy mutts told Cletus."

"Was Persephone that strong of a force to keep them from attacking Gravers Junction?"

"She was. And not just in our little town. She rode out and checked on the ones who chose to live outside of Gravers Junction."

"Why would they choose to live out there? With all the dangers and risks? I mean, I get why Booker can do it—he's a werewolf and can take care of himself. But why wouldn't people want to live here?" The answer scares me, and I don't know why. Maybe because there's something here Maureen or Garrett hasn't told us about that people don't want to be a part of. Like a cult of some kind. I stare into Garrett's kind eyes, and my gut tells me it's nothing like that. He's definitely keeping secrets, but I can't see him willingly wanting to hurt anyone. Maureen—eh, the jury is still out on that lady.

I lean forward over the railing and glance at the back hallway. This puts me mere inches from his face. He smells of fresh hay. Facing forward, our eyes lock and I put some distance between us. "Sorry, I was just seeing if supper's ready."

"You don't have any reason to apologize." There's a slight tick in his jaw, and I can't tell why he's so tense. I'm about to step down the rest of the stairs when he grabs my hand. "You don't have to choose this life, Bex. You can return to your farm—to a safe life where you can go outside at night and not worry about monsters or if you'll survive another day."

Not pulling away from his hand, I step off the last tread and come around to him. "Why do any of you stay?"

He sucks in a deep breath through his teeth. "It's complicated."

"You don't trust me?"

"I don't know you," he quickly clarifies.

I smile at him. "I think you know me more than most. You saw me with no clothes on—twice."

This makes him laugh. "That Spirit of the Land did a number on you. You're like a whole new woman!"

"You have no idea," I tease. The last time I flirted with a man was with Levi, and oddly I don't feel any guilt or shame about wanting more of it from Garrett. "But I still want an answer. Why do you stay in Gravers Junction?"

His laughter fades, but his smile lingers. "My family is tied to this town. This will always be my life, whether I want it or not."

More secrets. And I know there's no point in asking his meaning. I'm a stranger to these people. I may possess the dustslinger powers, but he's made it clear that isn't enough to earn their trust. "Did Cletus know about Booker and Persephone?"

"Yeah. I think everyone in Graveyard Territory knew about those two. It was also widely known that going after Booker to get to Persephone was off the table. No one wanted the wrath of the dustslinger at their front door," Garrett admits with a sigh. "Cletus will sympathize with Booker regarding his loss. It's why Book never took a pack. Choosing a commitment or a pack that's not with other werewolves is treason in their world."

"Treason?" I reiterate. "What was his punishment for loving Persephone? Besides not being allowed to have a pack."

"Death."

My insides go rigid. I glance toward the back hall, where I know Booker sits with Maureen, eating stew. Curiosity nips at my tongue, and I can't hold back. "Why didn't they kill him?"

"Because Cletus and Booker are family. Their fathers were brothers."

We walk toward the back hallway as he continues. "Booker's what you'd call a drifter. Those who are banished by force or leave of their own accord. Booker chose the latter. He fell in love, and"—Garrett pauses and stares into my eyes—"their love was that deep, unconditional kind where nothing else but the other person matters. They both sacrificed a lot to be with one another. Supposedly, Cletus and Booker were close in their youth, and Cletus knows what it's like to be forced to choose between the pack and love—because a long time ago when he had to face the same crossroads as Booker did, Cletus chose the pack."

I have so many questions. About pack laws, about Cletus and his love—where is she now? And about Booker's life as a drifter. Was it worth it? What happens now that Persephone's gone? Can he return to the pack?

"You're a curious one, aren't you?" Garrett asks. "I can tell you're trying to understand all of this. Take my word, you're going to need more than one night to absorb the inner workings of Graveyard Territory." He pauses and then adds, "If you decide to stay."

I stop walking and say, "So, what you're telling me is that I'll need to extend our visit a bit longer if I want to make an informed decision about picking up my life and moving here permanently."

He stops too and slowly turns to me. "Yeah. That's what I'm saying."

We stand there, waiting for the other one to speak. It's as if we're both trying to figure out what the other one is trying to really say without having to say any words.

Murphy interrupts the silence by poking his head out of

the back hallway. "Hey, you two coming to eat? I imagine we don't have much time before the show starts."

When I move to follow Murphy, Garrett grabs my arm, gently drawing me back to him. "Bex, you should know this isn't the kind of place to find love. So, if you stay, you need to be prepared to give that up. Booker gave up his family to have love. And look where that got him. He's alone now. And I highly doubt his family will welcome him back. I can't reckon I'd ever choose love, not when there's so much to lose in these parts."

His words sting. Maureen warned Nina and me about his position on love and how he's sworn it off. And here he is, telling me to my face, confirming what she said was true.

"That's your opinion," I say, trying not to stutter. "Sometimes a person can't help what they feel when it comes to matters of the heart. And denying those feelings only makes you want a person even more."

"Is that right?"

"I guess we'll find out, won't we," I say with a playful tone. "Now, I'm hungry. Let's go get some of Ruby's stew."

SIXTEEN

BEX

With most seats taken, I take a seat next to Booker, who sits next to Maureen in her usual spot at the head of the table. Nina isn't there. So, where the hell is she? Garrett comes in and sits at the other end of the table, opposite the woman who runs things in this town. Ruby's quick to set bowls of steaming stew in front of him and then me. I politely thank her, and before I can ask where my sister is, she hurries off.

Sheamus, the pianist, sits on my other side, and he's talking to Davie about how he loves music and how everyone should learn to play the piano. I chuckle when Davie argues he'd rather be a deputy like his dad than sit around and play "them ivory keys."

"What I do is important for this town," the old man argues. His rough hands clutch his spoon like it's a weapon.

"I didn't say it wasn't," Davie argues. "We all have to

play our part in keeping the town safe. I just don't see myself doing it from behind a piano."

Sheamus mumbles words I can't understand before shoveling another spoonful into his mouth.

"Come on, boy," Murphy says, standing from his seat. He gives a nod to Maureen before leaving the dining room. Davie follows, leaving his empty bowl on the table.

Shortly after, Booker and Garrett also leave, telling Maureen they're going to secure the barn and make sure the animals are all locked up.

I hop over into Booker's seat and tell Maureen, "I know you're upset with me, but I need to know how my sister's doing. Do you know where she is?"

She wipes her mouth with her cloth napkin and shakes her head. "She's been hanging out in the barn a lot. Other than that, I don't know where she is right now."

"What?!" I sit upright in the spindle chair. "What if someone or *something* took her?"

"Nobody took her," Maureen says under her breath, sounding a little annoyed.

Sheamus stands just as Ruby returns with her oversized tray. He looks to Maureen, and says, "Song number three?"

Maureen nods. "Yup. Song number three."

"Yes, ma'am." He shuffles by the empty chairs and heads out into the parlor.

Setting my napkin on the table, I abruptly stand, ready to leave too. "I need to go and find my sister."

"You aren't going anywhere. Cletus will be here any minute, and I can't have you disappearing."

Oh, I'll show her how I can disappear. But before I can, Ruby chimes in, saying, "Oh, hey! Are you asking about your sister?" She doesn't pause in talking to us while piling the dirty dishes onto her tray. "Oh, well, I saw her this morning. She borrowed a tray, filled it up with a day's worth of food, a small pot of coffee, and two large jars of water, and then disappeared from the kitchen before I could ask what she was up to. I assumed she needed some time to herself, maybe out in the barn with the horses."

"No one has checked on her after that?"

Maureen stands from her seat. "There aren't many places to hide in town, and if she wandered off out into the prairie, well, she knows better than to be out there past dark. So, I imagine she'll turn up at some point." Then to her friend, she asks, "Can you finish cleaning up later and go make sure the cage is hot?"

Ruby stops loading up her tray. "Good idea! Be right back!"

From out in the parlor, a series of sharp, rapid notes resolves into a faint piano melody.

Before I can ask how Ruby plans to charge the cage that encloses the garden and animal pens, Garrett's voice floats in from the hallway. "Hey! We've got company!"

Maureen gives me an eye roll and says, "Here we go. Come on, let's get this over with."

I hurry and follow behind her. Sheamus continues playing, like he's in his own little world, while Garrett and Booker stand at the front windows, looking out to the middle of town.

The sky has turned a dark blue, on the cusp of becoming night, and the waning moon sits off to the east, starting its rise and claim to the day. The dusk hour offers enough lingering daylight for the showdown that's about to go down. Two men and one woman riding horses stroll into town. More men and women with unruly hair and claws jutting from their fingernails follow on foot, surrounding the sides of the riders.

The burly rider in the middle calls out, "Come on out, Maureen! You know why I'm here!"

Maureen glances over at Sheamus. "Keep playing song number three, then use your judgment from there."

Sheamus nods and turns to his ivory and black keys. I don't recognize the song, but, even more importantly, I don't understand why they chose now to play music, as if this is some theatrical show we're all watching.

"Stay here," Maureen instructs me and then gives a stern glare to the sheriff. "Keep her in here. *If* we need her, then I'll call her."

Garrett nods. "Will do, ma'am."

Booker unlocks the latches, then opens one of the double doors. Maureen strolls outside, and Booker follows. They saunter off the wooden porch and down onto the dirt road. Garrett locks the doors and then returns to my side. He unlocks one of the windowpanes and pushes it open enough so we can hear their conversation.

"Hello, Cletus," Maureen shouts. "Been a while since you've visited Gravers Junction."

"It has," the man in the middle says with a snarl. He lifts a leg over the backside of his horse, who is also enormous.

I've never seen a breed that large before. Tufts of black hair on its legs fall around its hooves. Its dark mane is thicker than that of any horse I've seen, and its chest is broad, twice the size of Tumbleweed's. It's almost as if the horse were some kind of aberrant animal as well.

The man stands next to his massive horse, and I can see why he needs such a beast to ride. He must be well over seven feet tall. That poor horse, carrying around so much weight. He tips his black hat back, revealing dark creases embedded in the lines of his face. Long gray hair is tamed and tied at the back of his head, while a short, tidy beard covers the lower part of his face. His clothes and jacket are notably clean, in stark contrast to the rest of his pack, suggesting that his meticulous grooming habits may reflect his perception of what a superior should look like. If we weren't out in the middle of Graveyard Territory, I'd almost mistake him for a gentleman. Well, a rougher version of a gentleman.

"Where is she?" His voice is low and carries the weight of authority—most likely an earned authority through victories and bloodshed. Looking over the buildings of Gravers Junction, as if knowing the townsfolk are watching, he yells, "She has to pay for what she's done. Blood for blood, Maureen. One pup dead and one with a hole in her shoulder."

Maureen glances over at the inn, raising an eyebrow to me and Garrett. Then to Cletus, she shouts, "I wasn't aware blood had been spilled. I only recently heard about the encounter and was told it was just some of your *pups* playing rough with Booker." She gestures to the alpha wolf standing by her side.

Cletus doesn't look at his cousin. He holds his attention on the leader of Gravers Junction. "Blood, Maureen, now! Or I'll give the order. And I can't make any promises about damage control."

"You don't want to do that," Maureen says, no kindness in her voice. "Starting a war with Gravers Junction won't end well for you, or your reputation."

"What does that mean?" I whisper to Garrett.

"Out there"—he points to the plains beyond the town—"gossip spreads like wildfire. And if others get word of anyone showing signs of weakness, well, then they'll come for you. Just as Cletus has come here looking for you."

"I thought he's here because I broke some golden rule of interference." Which resulted in Garrett shooting and killing one of them while injuring another.

Garrett nods. "Yes, if you had minded your own business we wouldn't be in this situation. But what's done is done. And now he's here for blood retribution, and, I imagine, to test your weaknesses." I open my mouth to argue, but he quickly clarifies, "And before you ramble on about how strong you are, what I mean is you lack the experience to win against Cletus. And losing a fight out in these parts tells others you're weak."

I can't argue with that. We face the front window, watching and listening.

"Let the girl come out, say hello, and make her case for an apology. And then we'll see about leaving quietly." He waves a hand casually through the air as if this whole ordeal is one big inconvenience.

"What kind of apology are you looking for?" Booker

asks, as if he knows his cousin all too well and what he says isn't always what he means.

Cletus stares at Booker and Maureen. His gaze is predatory, and when his eyes briefly flash a golden yellow, the sand along my arms comes to life, rippling in anticipation.

"He's going to attack," I say, moving to the door. "They'll kill Maureen and Booker if we don't do something."

Garrett comes to my side, but instead of following me, he slams the door shut. "No. They know what they're doing. You're not in any position to go out there and save the day— not yet, anyway."

"I can fight!" I say with urgency, knowing there isn't time to argue. "The Spirit of the Land unlocked that knowledge within me. I know how to use my powers and fight."

"Dammit, Bex! How many times do I have to tell ya. You lack experience. Though, I'll admit you have heart." He crosses his arms over his chest, not backing down. "We sit this one out until Maureen calls for ya."

From out the open window, Book shouts, "Go home, Cletus!" His voice reverberates through the walls of the inn. "I won't tell you again."

Cletus narrows his dark eyes and inhales a deep breath, his body seeming to swell with the intake of air. This action triggers the surrounding werewolves to move in closer, growling in sync with their alpha. Then, something catches Cletus's attention as his gaze shifts from Maureen and Booker to over near the barn. I have to move to the other side of the parlor, to the other front window to see. Stepping out of the shadow of the barn, into the moonlight, is a giant wolf.

His thick, dark fur blends in with the night. Walking next to the giant wolf, in her favorite white dress dotted with tiny blue flowers, is Nina.

"No!" I say, but Garrett's arm catches around my waist. With no thought, I pull myself inward, disappearing from his grasp in a dust cloud, only to reappear across the room by the bar. "Don't touch me!" I say with a sharp snap. "I'm going outside."

"Please, just wait a damn minute! Your impatience is going to get them all killed!" he snarls, then tries to reel it in with a few deep breaths. Holding up two defeated hands, he pleads, "Two minutes. Give Maureen and Booker two minutes."

I could easily dust by him if I wanted, but something inside my gut doesn't want to betray him—doesn't want to cause any more tension between us. So I oblige, and stand by him at the window, praying Nina knows what she's walking into.

"Well, hello there. You're a pretty little thing." Cletus steps around the front of his massive horse, eyeing my sister like his next toy. "What's your name?"

Maureen and Booker turn to see what's caught Cletus's attention. Maureen quickly steps between Cletus and Nina. "Hey, they have nothing to do with why you're here. It's the dustslinger you're here for."

"Wait, what?" I whisper, stunned by Maureen's efforts to redirect the alpha's attention back to me.

"How is that possible?" Garrett leans his face closer to the glass pane, glaring out at my sister and the giant wolf by her side. Then to me he asks, "Who is your sister? What kind of aberrant is she?"

I shake my head and say, "She's not! She's…well, she's Nina!" Then I think about the whispering winds. "I-I don't know," I answer honestly. "She's always had a connection to the wind."

He shakes his head and rubs the top of his forehead. "You've got to be kidding me. Pale blonde hair, porcelain skin, and talks to the wind—dammit, I should've known. Come on," he says, grabbing me by the arm and pulling me outside. "Lock the doors, Sheamus!" Garrett commands before closing the door behind him.

The sound of one metal latch sliding into place after another knocks hard from inside the inn. Garrett walks over to where Booker stands, and I follow.

Booker briefly glances in our direction, then does a double-take. "Ah, shit. What are you two doing out here?" He doesn't sound pleased to see us.

"That's my sister," I say, pointing to Nina.

Cletus is out in the middle of the dirt road, eyes locked on my sister. His pack slowly moves to flank his sides, yet keeps a respectful distance, giving their alpha the space he needs.

A rush of wind blusters through town, blowing dust up into the night air. Some werewolves lose their hats, the wind tossing them off a few feet. Then, as if she commanded it, the wind rushes at her and the wolf, forcefully blowing her braids off her shoulders. Normally she closes her eyes and listens to whatever the whispering winds tell her, but not this time. Her eyes remain open and focused on the intruders.

"The winds tell me you don't belong here," she shouts, her voice sounding so much louder than I've ever heard her yell before.

She doesn't know they're werewolves, so I yell, "Nina! Run! Get out of here!"

"Yes, Nina," Cletus repeats with a chuckle, "run for me."

The giant wolf by Nina's side growls, showing its pristine white teeth and long canines. She strokes the wolf's fur, her hand moving along its raised hackles. "I don't think I will."

Maureen holds up her arms, her palms facing Cletus. "No! Please. Don't do this, Cletus!"

He finally looks away from my sister to Maureen, tsking at her. "You've been hiding a rogue werewolf. That in itself is a good enough reason for me to tear this town to the studs!" he growls.

"It's Hunter," she admits, keeping her hands up. "It was an accident. He was in the wrong place at the wrong time."

Booker looks over my head to Garrett. "Well, the werewolf's out of the bag."

Garrett's face is tense, a tick in his jaw as he stands by and watches what we're watching out in the center of town. "This isn't going to end well," he mutters, and I can see his gaze moving over the werewolves spreading out. "They're just waiting for his word," Garrett says to Booker. "They're actually going to tear the town down."

"Your blacksmith got all those metal sheets up, right?" Booker asks under his breath, trying not to draw any attention our way.

"Yeah," Garrett answers.

"That'll buy some time. Let's just hope Cletus is in a forgiving mood. Stay here," Booker says with a string of curses under his breath, slowly making his way out toward Maureen.

I can't just stand here, and step out to follow Booker, but Garrett grabs my arm and shakes his head. "Don't stir the pot," he warns.

"The winds tell me you don't belong here," Nina calls out again. Hunter continues to growl, stepping forward but staying close to Nina's side. My sister looks to the wolf, and then to Maureen. "He doesn't want to go with them," she tells her.

"You can speak with him?" she asks, her voice frail, as though the weight of the news has weakened her.

Nina shakes her head. "The winds speak with him, and the winds speak to me."

Maureen must realize something, which I'm guessing is the same something Garrett realized inside the inn when I mentioned how Nina can speak to the winds. Maureen briefly glances over at Garrett before telling Nina, "Hunter needs to know that Cletus will force him into his pack if he doesn't willingly pledge to an alpha."

Nina nods and closes her eyes. The air in the center of town swirls along the ground, rising up in the air. It then sweeps through the town, blowing at the horses' manes and the werewolves' unruly hair. This time, the werewolves standing about know to hold on to their sunrider hats. After a few heartbeats, she opens her eyes. "It's done. He knows."

I look to Garrett. "Why can't he pledge loyalty to Booker?"

Garrett shakes his head. "Booker was cast out, banished through a majority ruling by the alpha pack leaders. If he does, he and Hunter forfeit their lives. And Booker's family relations to Cletus won't save him again."

"But when it comes down to it…Hunter *can* pledge loyalty to Booker? There's no magical power preventing him from doing so, right?" I ask, still trying to understand the rules of this land.

"If he wants to risk every werewolf coming for his life and Hunter's life, then yeah, it's possible."

"Ugh. This is bullshit!" The curse feels good on my tongue. "There's got to be something you can do!"

Booker looks over his shoulder to us from where he's standing out in the middle of the road next to Maureen, eyeing us as if he can hear everything we're saying. Good to know, werewolves have excellent hearing.

"He can pledge loyalty to me!" Booker calls out. This causes the surrounding werewolves to growl, showing their disapproval.

Cletus faces his cousin. "By what right? You know you gave up pack rights when you left for that dirty dust whore."

"Call her that again, and I'll rip your throat out." Booker seethes as his fingers splay at his sides. Deliberately, his fingernails grow, extending out into monstrous claws.

"Ah, that's right. Didn't Malik take care of your little pet dustslinger? I heard he's got a weapon that she couldn't heal from."

One of Cletus's werewolves pulls out a revolver from its holster and pretends to shoot the werewolf standing next to him, yelling, "Bang, bang, bang," to emphasize the theatrics.

The werewolf feigns being shot, shuddering with each *bang* said and pressing a clawed hand to his chest. When their mocking dies down, Cletus laughs, revealing his sharp canines resembling something I'd imagine a vampire's fangs would look like. The alpha scowls and says, "One week." Then he repeats his promise to Maureen. "You have one week to say your goodbyes. Then the rogue wolf is mine."

While Maureen pleads for him to reconsider, Cletus looks up at the woman rider, and she nods, pointing a slender finger straight at Nina.

Oh, shit. What's happening now? Why is she pointing at my sister?

Cletus turns to Maureen, and adds, "And the girl. My witch wants the girl."

Witch? First werewolves, and then the knowledge that there are vampires out there… But now witches too?

Taking my sister from me is out of the question. Without thinking, I rush into the street from behind Garrett. He tries to grab me, but I pull myself inward, leaving nothing but a dust cloud for him to grasp at. I reappear a few feet from Cletus, his massive form towering over me.

Cletus narrows his dark eyes and laughs. "Ah, this must be the new dustslinger."

"I am!" I say as I feed the sand within me with determination and rage. Long ropes made of sand extend out from my wrists. The power flowing through my body feels like a sandstorm ready to explode. Bands of sand and dust rotate around my wrists and forearms, connected to the sandropes at my sides. I grip the lines and whip them out into the night air, a loud *snap* from each cracking in the air. The werewolves close in around Cletus, growling in defense and ready to defend their alpha. But he calls them off, more amused than fearful.

"We will have our dance, don't you worry, dustslinger.

But not tonight. For now…" He lunges at me with such speed he's on top of me before I can make myself vanish. With strong hands, he's pinned me to the ground. His weight is ten times heavier than the werewolf that attacked me last night. I try to pull myself inward, escaping in one of my dust clouds, but I can't transport myself away from him.

What the hell?

He leans closer, his glowing yellow eyes searching my face. Voices are shouting from all around, except I can barely hear them. They sound so far away. Looking over the beast's shoulder, I see some kind of shell, like a giant soapy bubble over us. Then, to my right, the witch sits up on her horse, one arm stretched out with her fingers splayed open as she whispers words I can't hear.

"You'll learn soon enough, but I'll clue you in now. My pack isn't like the other packs in Graveyard Territory. I've got a few outside aberrants in my pocket. That's Viola, my faithful witch with a hearty appetite, who likes to play with her food before devouring their essence. It's quite disgusting to watch, even for me."

He leans back but still holds me pinned to the dirt. "Viola has perfected this bubble to prevent you from using your powers. The old dustslinger figured out how to avoid Viola's magic—but you're fresh and don't know shit about these parts." He smiles, showing off his sharp teeth. Saliva spills from the corner of his mouth and onto my neck. The slimy, wet feeling trickles down along my collarbone. I want to scream and punch and…and cry. He could end my life right now if he wanted. Why had I let my emotions and impatience get the better of me?

"Now, I said I would give Maureen one week. Should I rescind that and take the wolf and your sister tonight?"

Shaking my head, I plead with him, "No. Please, no."

"You won't get any more mercy from me in the future. I think you've used up all of your…" His face contorts into a mocking one and he says with a childlike voice, *"I'm new to all this."* His expression hardens, and his eyes glow bright. "You have one week to say your goodbyes."

I'm about to nod, to agree to whatever this asshole wants, but the bubble around us pops and he's up on his feet so fast and assessing the attack. I roll onto my side and search out the witch. She's on her back a few feet away on the dirt road, rolling onto her side as if the air got knocked out of her chest.

"You touch my sister again and I'll kill you!" Nina shouts.

"No!" I shout, my voice still finding purchase in my throat. The fear of Cletus on top of me is taking longer to shake off. "Run, Nina! Get away!"

"You're going to pay for that," Cletus says, seething between gritted teeth.

"No!" Viola coughs, as she calmly gets to her feet. She hobbles over and rests a hand on Cletus's shoulder. His chest is heaving with deep breaths as he rages from my sister's attack on his witch. His claws are fully extended, and his feet are poised to lunge at my sister.

"Not tonight," she says, sliding her hand down his arm, then holding him at the elbow. She positions herself directly in front of him, not apparently angered by my sister's attack. His yellow eyes lock onto her face, and I wonder if he'll listen or toss her aside. I pray she has some kind of sway over the alpha prepared to spill blood.

"It's too easy tonight, and where's the fun in that?" She drags her long black nails across his chest. "I say, give 'em the week."

His heaving breaths ease up, and eventually he nods. They stare at one another as if speaking through their minds before he finally turns away. The witch spins on her toes and marches over to Nina. Hunter bares his teeth, growls, and creeps to intercept, except Viola lifts him off the ground and holds him suspended in the air with one of her bubbles.

Damn, this lady is powerful.

While holding the wolf a good distance away, Viola approaches Nina. I struggle to get to my feet, wanting to rush over and protect my sister, but my spine and tailbone ache from being thrown back to the ground when Cletus lunged at me. The witch whispers something in my sister's ear. Then, when she backs off, Nina simply nods. Viola turns and saunters away. As she walks by me, she doesn't even acknowledge me, as if I'm no threat to her.

Who's the alpha in this pack?

Cletus whistles, and Viola takes to her horse. The pack and two riders head out of town while Cletus lingers. "Seven days, Maureen. I'll be back to take what's mine." His giant of a horse turns, its hooves pounding against the dirt road, as he saunters out of Gravers Junction.

I want to burst into tears. Not only because of embarrassment at my actions but also because the countdown starts now, and in seven days, I may lose my sister forever.

SEVENTEEN

BEX

"Nina!" I shout and hobble my way toward her. She turns from the oversized wolf by her side and jogs, meeting me halfway. Our arms wrap around one another, and we squeeze, tears streaming down my cheeks. "I thought they were going to take you."

"I thought so too," she says softly, exhaustion weighing heavy in her voice. Leaning away, still holding on to me, she explains, "When the piano music started playing, Hunter reacted as if something dangerous was coming."

"You heard Sheamus playing the piano from underground?"

"There're pipes behind the piano that lead underground to different parts of our hidden community." Maureen comes over, keeping a watchful eye on the wolf, hesitant to get too close. "It's our way of letting those underground know what's happening up here."

"Clever," I admit.

"Hunter, can you hear me?"

The wolf stays perfectly still, staring up at the woman.

Nina breaks away from my embrace and runs a hand over his thick fur. "He hears you, but things aren't as clear. I've tried to help as much as I can, so his mind isn't completely lost in the dark. It's like when you talk to a dog—they only know certain words and the rest sounds like a foreign tongue."

A warm breeze sweeps over us, swirling around Nina, gently rippling the bottom hem of her dress. Then it rushes over me before hitting Maureen. The older woman's loose brown hair streaked with gray flutters for a second as the air swirls around her.

Maureen reaches out as if to touch the winds themselves. When the winds fade, she looks to my sister. "Was that them?"

"Yes," Nina answers. "They're also the ones that led me to him." She kneels beside the giant wolf, stroking the top of his back. "I didn't realize he was a werewolf at first. But then we met in a dream, and Hunter explained his situation."

"Did he?" Maureen holds a hand out to the wolf. Hunter turns away and heads back to the barn. Swallowing her pride, she nods and says, "I miss my son."

"Hunter is your son?" I rub my back, the ache growing into what I know will be a sizable bruise.

Maureen doesn't answer. Instead, she offers Nina her gratitude with a small smile before turning on her heels and heading over to where Booker and Garrett stand.

"What were you thinking?" I ask in a tone more scolding than curious. Then, not wanting to sour the mood, I think about what Nina must be feeling right now. It appears she's formed a bond with the wolf, and if that's important to her, then it's important to me too. "So, why isn't Hunter in human form like the other werewolves?"

Nina shrugs. "I don't know why he's stuck in this wolf's body. Something we've yet to figure out, I guess." She loops her arm through mine and says, "You know, it would be easier for us to take our horses and ride home. Avoid any of this bloodshed."

We start walking toward the inn. I pat my sister's arm, agreeing with her. "We could, and be done with this place. We delivered Persephone's message, and I've got what I need in regard to this magic inside me."

Nina doesn't look at me; she stares straight ahead. Her voice holding a weight of sorrow as she asks, "So we leave tomorrow?"

"Do you want to leave?" I already know I don't, but if she does I would understand.

"I'd rather not be claimed and towed off by a malevolent alpha werewolf in seven days."

"If you leave, they'll eventually find you." Booker comes over and meets us on our way to the inn. "They've got your scent. And I think that witch has a special interest in you, which means they'll come for you wherever you hide."

I look at Nina. She's in danger either way. Whether we stay or whether we go. "So, we stay," I suggest, hoping she understands our chances are better here with people who understand the ways of this land. "Maybe not permanently, but for now…we stay."

Nina squeezes my hand perched on her arm. "We stay.

But I'd like to return to our home and collect some of our belongings. There's something there I want that I think I'll need in the days to come."

I stop right before the wood platform. "Okay, then we ride home and come—"

"No. I'll ride home, and you stay here and learn more about how to control your powers. We have seven days before Cletus returns. That means I can leave tomorrow and be back just in time."

"No!" I protest, but Maureen's quick to cut in and say, "I'll send a few of the sheriff's deputies to accompany you."

"Thank you," Nina says, then starts walking toward the barn. "I'm going to check on Hunter. Don't wait up!"

"Wait!" I protest. "I don't want to part ways again."

This time it's Garrett who speaks as he walks by us, heading to the barn with Nina. "No. You stay here. We have a lot to go over—about the laws of this land." He's too far gone for me to argue with him, and I think that's exactly what he wanted. To say his piece and not give me a chance to argue. Damn him.

"Booker"—Maureen turns to her friend—"would you mind staying for a few more days?"

"How about I stay the week?" he counters.

"That would be lovely. Come on, let me show you to your room," she says, walking away. I'm left alone, everyone heading inside. Maureen calls to me, "You best not stay out here. One evil has left town, but there are others lurking in the shadows waiting for the right opportunity to strike."

Not wanting to find out what she means, I hurry to follow her and Booker into the inn. Glancing over my shoulder, I catch Garrett staring at me as he closes the barn door shut. I want to go with Nina, yet I also want to spend some time with the sheriff. Dammit. One day I'll have the intimidation and respect that Persephone had, and then no one will question my decisions.

I sit at one of the empty tables in the parlor while Maureen shows Booker upstairs to his room. The piano music comes to an abrupt stop before Sheamus plays another slow melody. Curious, I move to the piano's side and search for these pipes.

"You won't see the pipes unless you move the piano." His voice is hoarse. Thin strands of white hair cross over the bald spot on top of his head. Age spots speckle his pale face while small spectacles rest on the tip of his nose.

"Where do they lead?"

"Did Miss Maureen tell you about the pipes?" he inquires with a narrowed gaze. The skin around his eyes pinches, and there's a faint haze shrouding his brown irises.

"Yes, she did."

He nods, as if disappointed. "Well, then"—he continues playing his soft melody—"the pipes go to various parts of the community below. It's our way of alerting people of danger or the sun's setting, or the arrival of a guest. Each song has its own meaning."

"What does this one mean?" I ask, trying to identify the tune but failing.

"Oh, this one—means all is safe. The next one I'll play will tell everyone to settle down in their homes for the night."

"Clever," I admit. "And what happens if you're not here to play the music?"

"There are a few others whom I've taught to play. In case something happens to me."

Lowering myself into the wooden chair next to the piano, I say, "This place sure is impressive. I mean, I have no idea how you get fresh water out here or where you get rations and supplies, but you all have thought of everything to keep the dangers out and the town safe."

A smile spreads across the old man's face. The music ends, and with a wink, he jumps right into playing the next tune. I'll need to look about more closely the next time I'm down in the tunnels to see if I can spot the other end of the pipes.

"You ready for bed?" Nina asks, stepping out from the back hallway door. "I'm exhausted and want to get a good night's sleep before we leave in the morning."

I stand and rest a hand on Sheamus's shoulder. "Good night, and I look forward to hearing you play more tomorrow."

"Good night, Miss Rebecca."

"Bex is fine."

"Yes, well then, good night, Miss Bex."

Before I can correct him again, not needing the *Miss* part, I give in and follow Nina up the stairs. We pass by Maureen and Booker quietly talking in his guest room, and when she sees us, she moves past him and closes the door. No *good night* or *talk to you tomorrow*. Just closes the door as if she can't deal with us right now. Though, it's probably more me than Nina. Nina has helped bring Maureen closer to her son and may even help Hunter shift out of his wolf state. I, on the other hand, keep messing up—making things worse. Maybe Garrett is right. My staying behind gives me more time to learn the laws of this land. I want to do right—to save my sister from that heathen Cletus but also do my part to protect the townsfolk from other aberrant threats.

Inside our bedroom, Nina's already heating a giant bucket of water. The pump in the back corner is quite convenient rather than going outdoors and lugging heavy buckets of water up three flights of stairs. It'll take some time to get a full tub of hot water, so in the meantime, I browse through the books shelved on the narrow bookcase.

"They've got some classics and some I've never heard of."

Nina doesn't answer. When I look over my shoulder, she's at the window, staring down.

"What is it?" I ask, hoping there isn't anything evil lurking outside.

"This wasn't what I was expecting to find out here in Graveyard Territory."

I'm about to pluck a book from the shelf but leave it to address her concerns. "I shouldn't have lied to you about why we were coming out here."

She doesn't seem to hear my apology and instead says, "When I was a kid, and I made my escape from the north, I traveled this land, hearing the screams at night. The winds guided me to where I could rest and hide from being a victim of whatever evil was causing those screams. Yet, every moment I was out here, I swear I felt a familiar presence trying to call me—needing me to rescue them. I could've searched harder to find whoever it was, but I was too scared."

I stand next to her at the window. "The winds saved you, Nina. If you had wandered off to find the mysterious person or thing that beckoned you, well then, you might have never found our farm. And that means you wouldn't be my sister."

This snaps her out of whatever trance holds her attention. "I never thought of it like that."

"You survived the worst of the worst out here and found your way into our life. Now much older and wiser, we've returned to the land that once beckoned you. Maybe it was meant to be this way. Our being here together."

"Maybe." She goes to the bucket, checks the temperature, and then dumps the water into the copper tub. A few more bucketfuls and it'll be full. She fills up another bucket from the water pump in the corner while I find clean towels folded on the dresser. "The winds tell me we're safe here, but there's something else here that makes me feel like we're not safe—that we're exactly where we shouldn't be. There's something in this town that everyone out in Graveyard Territory wants."

"That makes sense, especially given there's a town full of people who don't have to live out here. They must be here for a reason."

Setting the bucket of water onto the iron stove, Nina nods. "And that's what we need to find out before we decide about staying here on a longer-term basis. What secrets is Maureen hiding about this town?"

Despite the room's increasing warmth, I want a steaming hot bath, so I add more chopped wood into the stove and then shut the iron gate.

"What did the witch whisper to you tonight?" I ask.

Nina perches on the edge of the copper tub and says, "She told me not to run. She said she's been waiting a long time for…" Her words trail off, as if she needs to choose them carefully. Then she sniffles before continuing, "For me. She said with me, we might be able to stop the ancient evil trying to claim this land."

"What? That doesn't make any sense."

She sighs. "Nothing makes sense out here, Bex."

She's not wrong about that.

"We'll figure it out. One step at a time."

"After my bath, I want you to tell me everything that happened while you were out there." She gestures with a nod toward the window. "I saw you call on your power tonight—those amazing sandropes. I want to hear all about how you figured out how to do that."

A chuckle escapes. "I'll happily tell you everything. Even the part where I had to get naked in a hot spring deep in a cave with Garrett."

This brings a wicked smile to Nina's face. "What?! Oh, yes, you must tell me everything!"

"I will. But right now, you soak in the tub while I pick out a book to read."

With a nod, she pours the last bucket into the tub and then undresses. I give her some privacy and return to the bookshelf. Instead of taking one of the classics, I drag my fingers along the spines until I reach one that isn't familiar to me: *Energies from Beyond.*

What are energies from beyond? The opening lines read, *All mystical elements originate from the ley lines that cross over from the beyond into our real world. It's these pure energies that are the origins of life to aberrants.*

I take the book over and lie in bed, absorbing the words on the pages, learning more about a secret world that hides in plain sight from the rest of the world. These ley lines must be somewhere in Graveyard Territory, breached over from some other world beyond. The list of questions grows longer and longer about whether we belong in this world or the naïve one that doesn't know aberrants exist.

EIGHTEEN

BEX

The next morning, I stand outside the inn, the heat of my coffee seeping through the tin cup into my palms. The morning is cool, though I know the sun will soon warm the land.

Out in the center of town, four horses are hitched to the stagecoach. Murphy and his son, Davie, load supplies for the trip. I walk over and stop beside Murphy while Davie moves down the line of horses, tugging leather straps, testing chains with his boot, then bracing both hands on the long wooden beam that runs between them. He rocks it once, listening for the faint *clink* of iron. Satisfied, he nods to his father.

"All set for the ride out?" I ask.

"Yeah. With four horses, we'll make good time. Maureen doesn't like leaving the town with no horses, so we rarely hitch four. But since your two are here, she said we could take them."

I sip my coffee, trying to understand his meaning.

"I don't reckon it'd be a good idea to flee on a horse if danger comes to town. Though, you never know when you need to get somewhere fast." He tips his hat to me before hollering at his son. "Boy, what did I tell you about crossing the lines!"

"Sorry, sir." Davie works the reins so they're not tangled.

"Bex!" Nina calls from the open door of the inn. "Can you help me?"

I hurry over to the wooden planks of the porch area where Nina and Ruby are setting out crates filled with food, jars of water, and clean pots and pans. Maureen comes out after them holding a stack of blankets. We all bring the supplies to the stagecoach, where Murphy and Davie help load everything on top and inside the coach.

Garrett and a woman I recognize from the first day we arrived walk toward us. The woman has tan skin and wild red hair peeking out from beneath her sunrider hat. Garrett introduces her, saying, "This is Loretta. She's one of my deputies. She's also got the fastest draw that I've ever seen."

Loretta rests her hands on her pistols, snug in their holsters hanging on the thick belt around her waist. She yawns, then says, "I'm your night watch."

"She can't be too fast if she's half asleep," I say quietly to Nina.

The gunslinger hears me and spins to face the building next to the inn, whipping out both pistols. With a loud *bang-bang*, she shoots two shots at the cans perched on top of the roof. A faint stream of smoke escapes the end of each barrel. "We leave those up there for whenever someone needs a demonstration."

She holsters her firearms, then climbs inside the stagecoach and gets comfortable against the pile of blankets Maureen stashed on the bench seat. We all watch as Loretta kicks up her feet, crossing one pant leg over the other, and rests her boots on the opposite bench while tipping her sunrider hat down over her face. Unbound by her hat, short red curls now twist out in a wild, free style. "Wake me when I'm needed."

I don't dare whisper my thoughts aloud about how rude this woman is being, fearing she might have supernatural hearing or something.

"Well, we best be going," Murphy says to Nina. Davie climbs up on the driver's bench, adjusting his sunrider hat before tying a dust-catcher around his neck. Nina nods to Murphy, and the man climbs up to his seat next to his son's.

"Be safe," I say to Nina.

She pulls me in for a hug and whispers, "You too. Don't be a hero either. Stay alive and just learn as much as you can about this place. The more you know, the more you can teach me when I get back."

"Deal," I say and then squeeze her tight.

When we part, Garrett's there holding the carriage door open. Nina steps inside and sits next to a sleeping Loretta.

"I'm serious," Nina says, hanging her head out the open window. "Listen to Maureen and Garrett, and don't take any risks. I'll be back in six days."

"Love you!" I shout as Murphy snaps the reins and calls to the horses. The chains rattle and hooves pound the dry dirt.

Nina shouts back, "I love you too!"

"She's in good hands," Garrett says to me. "Murphy and his son have been going out visiting other towns for years. They have the entire Graveyard Territory mapped out in here," he says, tapping his forehead. "And if that ain't enough, Loretta is—"

"The fastest draw in all the land," I say, finishing his sentence.

"Yes, she is. But I was going to say fearless too. She'll run straight into danger with or without being told to."

I lower my tin cup, the coffee now cold. "How does one run straight into danger and not break the laws of the land?"

Garrett offers me a smile. "She knows the laws, so she knows when to charge and when to stay put. And when she charges, she commits. You can't have any doubts—not a single thought about why you're charging or what the outcome may be. Loretta is great at closing her mind off to wandering thoughts and doubts. She's as focused as they get." He walks past me and says over his shoulder as he makes his way to the barn, "I've got to tend to the horses, then I'll come and get you for today's lesson."

"Why can't I come with you?" I shout.

"Because we need to talk," Maureen says from behind me. She and Booker stand up on the platform porch in front of the inn. Booker sips his coffee while Maureen waves for me to follow.

Inside, Maureen and Booker sit at one of the empty tables in the front parlor. Sheamus stands from the piano and disappears into the back hall. Faint voices drift out from the back rooms, where I assume Sheamus and Ruby are conversing.

"What's this all about?" I ask, taking a seat at the small, round table.

"Garrett'll go over the laws of the land and the different supernaturals we have around, but we wanted to talk to you about why we're all doing this. Why we stay."

"I'm assuming it has something to do with ley lines," I suggest.

Booker leans back in his chair, cracking a smile and laughing while Maureen's eyes go wide. Between his amused laughter, he says, "Whelp, I wasn't expecting her to say that!"

"Quiet, Book," Maureen scolds her friend before narrowing those wide eyes into a glare, suspicion settling into her features.

"I read a book last night, well, started reading a book," I say, then pull out the small canvas-bound book I tucked into the pocket of my skirt. Maureen holds out a hand, and I place the book in her hand. "It's an odd book to have on the shelf, *Energies from Beyond*, and normally I wouldn't read any sort of propaganda like this, but out here in this territory it seemed fitting. So, you're protecting some kind of mystical energies, I assume."

"I'll be damned." Booker's words are still entangled with his chuckles. "This might be easier than you thought." He slaps a hand onto the table and then stands, taking his empty coffee cup and sunrider hat that's sitting on the table with him. "I'm going to see if Ruby has any leftovers before she feeds them to Davie's mutt outside."

Maureen's gaze softens, and she hands me back the book. "Keep reading it."

I pocket the small book, and when she gets to her feet and waves for me to follow, I do without question. She's not wearing a dress or skirt today, but a pair of men's pants. There's silence between us as I trail behind her into the inn's back storage room and down the stairs leading to the underground community. I don't think this part of Gravers Junction will ever get old with me, with how they've basically built an underground hidden town, leaving the buildings up top as a decoy.

Thinking about town above has me wondering if others know the truth about where the people of this town live. "Do others outside of Gravers Junction know about the homes and businesses connecting underground through a system of tunnels?"

"Some," she says indifferently. We've taken a few lefts and rights, and I've lost track of how to get back to the main stairs to the inn. We come to a dead end, which has been carved out into a quaint reading nook with two wingback armchairs, a small three-tier cart with jars of water and extra candles, a bookcase set against the wall between the chairs, and a woven rug to complete the cozy feel.

"Are we going to read more books about mystical energies?" I ask as Maureen approaches the bookcase.

"Not exactly," she says, then pushes the bookcase aside as if it were one of the barn doors, revealing a secret set of stairs. These, unlike the wood-framed ones leading to the underground tunnels, are carved into the earth, packed dirt forming the tread. "Watch your step," she says, striking a match and lighting a lantern waiting to be used on the inside wall. Once I'm through, and a few steps down, Maureen slides the bookshelf back into place. I'm not a fan of tight spaces, and I'm tempted to tell her there's no way I'm going any farther. But the stairwell is wide enough for three or four people to walk side by side, so the feeling of tight space doesn't overwhelm me.

"Stay close, and please watch your step." Maureen takes the lead, holding the lantern up. The stairwell curves, and we make our way deeper into the earth.

"How far does this go?" I ask after a few minutes. The temperature of the air has gotten noticeably colder, and I wish Maureen had offered me a sweater or something for the chill.

"I'd say we're about halfway down."

I don't ask, but I assume she's taking me to see the ley lines. The book described the energy as a myth—something no one had ever seen. If it existed, the author speculated that the energy would be so powerful that it would be untouchable. They estimated the power to be greater than a strike of lightning. There was also a chapter theorizing about harnessing such power, which is ridiculous. Men have been trying to bottle the energy from lightning for years now. Some things aren't meant to be controlled by man.

Yet here we are, descending into the depths of the Earth to what I'm assuming are these ley lines. More questions form as we proceed in silence. How did the author of the book know to call the phenomenon *ley lines*? How was the ley line beneath Gravers Junction discovered? Why are Maureen and the town hiding it?

When we reach the bottom landing, Maureen continues forward through a wide tunnel. The light of the lantern guides us through the darkness. There are several tunnels that branch off, and she even takes a few of them.

"You sure you know where you're going?"

"It's up ahead," she says, then recesses the wick of the lantern until the glow of the light dies completely.

My heartbeat picks up, not particularly keen on being so deep underground…in complete darkness…where we could easily get turned around and lost. I suck in deep breaths of cold air, trying to keep my rising panic at bay. I'm about to cry out for Maureen when I see it up ahead. A faint glow of light. It's not like lantern light with its warm glow reaching the walls of the tunnel. It's more like the moonlight that reflected off the hot spring beneath the rock formation at Booker's place. A soft, pale light that barely reaches a hand's width.

"Is that it?" My nerves relax, as my curiosity takes over.

"Mmh," she hums. "Come on." I trail behind her, captivated by her silhouette as it stands out against the glow of the pale blue light and blends in with the surrounding shadows.

As we get closer, it's more apparent that the glow of light is coming from around the corner. Actually, the tunnel zigzags with tight turns, and the farther we move through it, the brighter the light becomes. At the end of the tunnel, we enter a cavern so large you could fit an entire town inside it.

"Maureen, this is amazing!" I gaze upward at the blue energy that's at least three stories above our heads. It resembles a colossal rope, shining with vibrant intensity while sparks of pale blue energy flicker off from its stream. There's also a faint hum coming from the energy line.

My dustslinging magic reacts to the energy, coming alive along my arms. The gritty sand grows warmer, as if I were standing out under the sun and absorbing the warmth and sunrays.

"You haven't seen the best part yet," she says. "See how the energy passes through that rock?"

I follow her pointed finger and see the rock she's speaking of. I thought the energy stopped at that point, but she's right. There's a hole in the center, and the stream passes through it.

Maureen weaves between tall stones jutting up from the cave floor until we've cleared the large boulder that's blocking our view to see the center of the cavern. The second we're on the other side, I gasp. "Whoa. What is that?"

Maureen leans against one of the tall boulders, tucking her hands into her front pockets. "There are ley lines all over the world. Most are invisible to the human eye, but here, because of the intersection of so many ley lines, and the lack of natural light, we're able to see them."

When she says *them*, I count the connecting lines. Six lines. And though they don't all cross at one direct intersecting point, they all cross one another in a beautiful lace pattern, like when a spider first starts its spiderweb.

"This is why you stay?" I say, my gaze following one line after the other, each disappearing into the cavern wall through its own hole. I wonder where the lines are traveling off to.

"Yes, this is why my family has stayed in Gravers Junction all these generations. It wasn't always our responsibility to protect the grandeur junction of lines. That's what they call a place where four or more ley lines converge. You see, a long time ago, way before this cavern was discovered, a man named Benedict Graves made a deal with an ancient demon stuck between worlds. The demon promised Benedict everlasting life and fortune beyond anything he could imagine if he searched the lands for a powerful source of energy that could free the demon from limbo."

I lean against a nearby rock, entranced with Maureen's story. I never heard anything so absorbing in any of my fiction books back home. "And I'm assuming Benedict—Wait, did you say Graves? As in Malik Graves?" I know the name since Persephone was so adamant that I remember it.

Maureen nods. "I'm getting to that part. And you're right, Benedict and his family did eventually find this cavern with the power source the demon wanted. Instead of returning to the demon and relaying the cavern's location, Benedict's son, Hershel, convinced his father to protect the power from the evil of Graveyard Territory. And they'd lived in the Graveyard Territory long enough to know they couldn't live in a normal home."

"Let me guess," I interrupt, wanting to see if my hunches are right before she divulges the truth. "They dug out the tunnels and their home beneath the ground and then built the town over it."

"Yes, that's exactly what they did. Except their numbers weren't big, so they didn't need the space we have today.

Hershel recruited some men and their families to come live out here and help build their secret town. I don't know how long it took, but they did it. And my great-grandfather was among the men recruited to help dig out the tunnels and protect the grandeur junction of lines."

It then dawns on me how the town's name came about. Gravers, the family that discovered the ley lines, and junction from grandeur junction of lines. Clever.

"When did protecting the ley lines become your family's charge?"

"Hershel's son, Malik, had different plans for Gravers Junction. But that's a story we can save for tonight, after supper. Just know that being a dustslinger—protecting this town—isn't about protecting the residents. It's about protecting this power from falling into the wrong hands. No matter what. Do you understand?"

I don't nod or say *yes*, and I don't disagree either. I'd been ready to say yes yesterday. But now, seeing the power they guard, and knowing every aberrant alive wants it, this is way more than protecting a town against retribution or random bandits. This town is always on alert. A threat can arrive at any time, intent on taking that power.

Part of me wants a normal life, which I thought could've been possible here, but now knowing it's about protecting this mystical energy…well, that changes everything. Now that the stakes are higher, I need a stronger reason to stay.

And there might be one handsome reason.

Or at least I hope there might be.

I think about what I'd told him by the stairs last night before supper: *Sometimes a person can't help what they feel when it comes to matters of the heart. And denying those feelings only makes you want a person even more.*

Maureen pushes off the boulder she's been leaning against. "If this power falls into the wrong hands, it's not just Graveyard Territory that will suffer."

Basically, whether I stay or go, there's a chance evil could find its way into Billingsworth County. The odds are better though, I imagine, if I stay. And Nina, since there's a strong magic within her too.

Not ready to commit to anything, I say, "Thank you for telling me the truth. You've given me a lot to think about."

She offers me an understanding smile before we make our way out of the cavern.

NINETEEN

BEX

The moment Maureen and I step out into the back hall of the inn, Ruby comes rushing out of the kitchen carrying her favorite tray. "Oh, hey there! Just in time for lunch. I've set up the picnic table for today's meal."

"Sounds perfect," Maureen says. "You go ahead, Bex. I'll be out shortly."

Ruby holds the tray with one hand over her shoulder while gesturing for me to go ahead with her free hand. Outside, the warm wind feels nice after being in the cold tunnels deep beneath the ground. Ruby veers right, and I follow.

Booker, Sheamus, and Garrett are there waiting for lunch to be served. I take a seat next to Booker at the picnic table, across from Sheamus, while Garrett sits in one of the rocking chairs nearby. The surrounding grass is worn through, leaving dirt patches, especially around the rocking chairs.

Gopher barks and wags his tail, trailing behind Ruby's feet. He's hungry too.

The rocking chairs are facing the open prairie, where the tall grass sways with the gentle, warm winds. It's beautiful and reminds me of the open plains behind my farm. There's something peaceful about seeing nothing but nature in its purest form.

"Come and get some food," Ruby calls to Garrett while the other two men grab their plates and pick sandwiches off the platter Ruby has carried outside. It's almost as if he didn't hear her, or is choosing to ignore her, but after a few brief moments, he stands and makes a plate and sits at the picnic table.

I grab a plate and pick out one of the ham sandwiches. Ruby turns to go inside, and I call to her, asking, "Aren't you eating with us?"

"Oh, I ate earlier! But thank you! I've got to get all the meats and cheeses back to the cold cellar before this heat spoils them." The petite woman and her wooden tray disappear inside.

A cold cellar to keep the food from spoiling. Huh, I'd like to see that one of these days. But I'll wait for Nina to get back, because I know she'll want to see that too.

Everyone eats in silence, except for Booker and Sheamus, who engage in small talk here and there. It's nice, and I can see why they consider themselves family, even if they aren't blood. Curious about the families that live here, I ask, "Where are all the children?"

This has all three men frozen in place. It's Booker who lowers his sandwich and explains, "This isn't the place for kids. There have been enough parents who've seen their kids get taken or killed over the years that, well…"

Garrett cuts in and finishes explaining, "We have a partnership with a town outside of Graveyard Territory. It's about half a day's ride east. When a woman is with child, we send the couple there until they're ready to return."

"No one is forced to stay here," Sheamus adds. "We do it for the greater good. Because we know what would happen to the world if the evils of this land had access to—"

"The grandeur junction of lines," I say before he can.

Sheamus nods.

"Regular folks too," Booker adds, staring at the old planks of the picnic tabletop as if lost in a memory. "Men can be just as dangerous as a vampire or a werewolf. In their own way."

"You're not wrong," I agree, knowing a few men in my time who enjoy holding power over folks who don't have it. I'm tempted to ride back east, to Seymour Heights, and find that Ambrose Redding and show him what actual power looks like. The sand in my forearms agrees as bands form, spinning around my wrists and forearms.

Booker mumbles a soft *yes* before taking another bite of his sandwich.

"You ready to learn more about the inner workings of Graveyard Territory?" Garrett asks, pushing his plate aside.

I finish the last bite of my ham sandwich and nod. He stands, and as I finish chewing, I get to my feet and collect our plates.

"Ruby will get them," he says, taking the plates from my hand and setting them on the table. "Believe me, keeping her busy is good for her. If she gets bored or sits still too long, well, then—"

"She turns to stone!" Booker interjects and then bursts out laughing. "Oh, I couldn't resist. Sorry, Garrett."

Sheamus joins in, laughing at a joke I don't understand. Garrett rolls his eyes and throws some ham to Gopher before walking out toward the tall grass of the prairie.

"Come on, Bex. We've got a lot to cover."

I like the way Garrett talks and explains things to me. He doesn't downplay information because I'm a woman. Or he sees me as another supernatural being, someone who needs to be self-reliant. I don't know. Whatever the reason, I like that he's forward with me about the laws of the land and the supernatural beings out here.

We've been talking for hours, and the sun dips closer to the horizon. The flat plains stretch far and wide in all directions.

"Come on, let's go help lock up the town for the night."

"Yes… That's something else I want to learn how to do. What is your nightly routine for reinforcing all the ways to get underground?"

"Hey! There you two are!" Ruby comes outside holding a basket looped through one arm. There's a rag folded over something inside. "Can I steal Miss Bex? I'd like to show her how I charge the garden cage each night."

A thrill zips through me, excited to learn how the cage keeps dangers out. "Oh, yes. I'd love to see that!" I exclaim without waiting for Garrett's approval. Picking up the front of my skirt, giving my feet more room to run, I hurry and follow Ruby around the side of the inn out to the center of town. "What's in the basket?" I ask, curious if it has anything to do with charging the cage.

"You'll see!"

We make our way between the two smaller single-story buildings out to her garden. The garden and animal coops are all inside the giant wire cage and stretch from behind the smaller building to halfway behind the barn. There's a side door to the smaller building, and she unlocks the padlock with a key from her apron pocket. "You're going to love this," she says with a playful giggle.

Inside is a large room filled with herbs hanging in bunches to dry out. This must be where she preps her spices. The air is filled with so many scents; I can only place a few. Nina would be better at identifying them. There's a shelf in the far corner with bowls lined inside and a rag gently resting over the top. Ruby sees me eyeing them and says, "Those are for tomorrow. It's dough that'll rise overnight."

"Ah," I say, realizing she's got a whole town to feed, and that's why there are so many.

"Over here," she calls to me. She stands against the back wall, next to a window that overlooks the garden. There's a wooden box nailed to the wall about the size of a sunrider hat. She unlatches the top and lifts it back. Inside is a glass sphere about the size of an apple. The back of the box is open directly to the metal cage outside, and when she picks up the glass ball and hands it to me to hold, I see a small metal plate where the item sat. I want to ask so many questions about it all, but I reel in my impatience and let her finish.

She reaches over onto the table and pulls her basket closer. Carefully, she unfolds the rag, and as she does, rays of pale blue light illuminate the space. With two hands, she lifts out another glass ball, except this one contains some kind of blue energy.

"Is that energy from the ley line?" I ask, trying to see every side of the glass sphere.

Ruby nods. "A friend of mine showed me how to trap some of the energy and use it to charge the metal cage."

I reach up to touch it, but she blocks my hand with hers. "You can't touch it!" Ruby's usual joyful and friendly manner has vanished, replaced by an undeniable seriousness. "It's basically lightning in a glass orb."

My brows pinch, and I stare at her bare hands handling the dangerous magic. "How are you able to hold it then?"

"Well, that's something else I should probably tell you. I was hoping Nina would be here when I explained where I come from, but I guess I can talk with her when she gets back."

Ruby sets the contained ley line magic into the box, and immediately blue sparks emit against the metal plate and nearby metal cage. "There we go! The cage is charged. If anyone touches it or tries to get to our garden and farm animals, well then, we'll find their dead body lying in the dirt the next morning."

"Lovely," I say with a sense of unease. I'd like to avoid that chore—cleaning up the charred remains of those who dare try to get past Ruby's death cage.

"I'm not exactly human," she confesses.

"I gathered that from your amazing strength. You're always carrying that huge tray with all those dishes and platters, and then when I saw you balancing that massive axe in the middle of the kitchen the other night, I knew something was up with you."

She laughs. "My people are called stonians. We're pretty much human, except for two things. The first is that our skin is stronger than any stone you've come across, which also gives me my aberrant strength. And second, my insides are like yours except a mirror version. So, my heart is over here." She taps the right side of her chest. "And my stomach's over here." Her hand drops, and she presses it to the right side of her torso.

I reach out and touch her hand. It's cool, and feels soft, like a human hand, except when I go to squeeze it, there's no fleshy push. The smooth skin feels like skin, except it's a stone version. "This is all a lot to take in," I admit. "First werewolves, then ley lines, and now people made of stone."

"You get used to it," she says while setting the empty glass ball into her basket, and we head out of her herb cabinet, as she likes to call it. After she locks the padlock, we quickly make our way over to the inn as the sun has pretty much set. I guess I'll watch someone else tomorrow night for another of the many ways they secure the town.

Inside the inn, Sheamus is at his piano, playing the evening tune. Ruby continues toward the kitchen, calling out to me, "See you in the morning!"

"Good night, Ruby!" I call back.

Garrett walks out from behind the bar, closing the bar hatch behind him. He strolls past me and starts up the stairs. "Are you coming?" he asks, and my heart flutters with uncertainty. Why are we going upstairs to the bedrooms?

I swallow, trying to find my words. "Sure," is all I whisper. I don't argue, or ask, or contemplate whether we should go upstairs. Whatever he wants to discuss or show me…or do…I'm ready for whatever lesson he's got planned.

TWENTY

BEX

He walks past 2B and heads up to the third floor. We're going to my room, and when we get inside, he shuts the door behind us and locks it. Confused, I move to the small bookcase and wait to see what he says or does, and why it has to be up here right next to my bed.

"I have to show you something," he says, and then goes to the locked closet door.

The sand stirs along my arms, so whatever's behind that door, the dustslinger within me also knows. I move closer, eager to learn more of Gravers Junction's secrets. After he unlocks the door, he turns and hands me the key. "I have a spare in case you lose this one. But try not to, okay?"

I take the long iron key and tuck it in the skirt pocket of my dress. I'll have to ask Ruby later for a piece of twine or ribbon so I can tie it around my neck. Inside is a dark hall, not a closet. He gestures for me to go first, and I do. Immediately to my left is a staircase. "Where does that go?"

"Up to the loft."

"Can I see what's up there?"

"You can, but later. After I've shown you Persephone's private study. Then, I'll leave you to explore wherever you want."

I stop at a closed door at the end of the short hallway. "Go ahead. It's unlocked," Garrett says behind me.

Turning the knob, I push the door open and step inside. The moon has barely risen, but it's enough to fill the room with a pale light. Garrett strikes a match from somewhere in the room, replacing the soft moonlight with a strong, warm glow from the oil lantern sconces affixed to the walls on opposite sides of the room.

Inside the room, there's a small writing table with an upholstered wingback chair behind it set below the window. Closest to us is another small bookcase full of books and stacks of paper. Then across the room, against the far wall is a large trunk with worn metal corners. Above the trunk are three outfits hanging on the wall like artwork being shown off. One is a dress similar to the ones I'm used to, with a top button collar, long sleeves, and a full skirt. The fabric is light brown with thin, dark vertical stripes. Normally, only the wealthiest women back in our old town could afford such fine fabrics as this for their dresses. The second and third outfits are quite similar. A white blouse, the neckline not as high as I'm used to, beneath a brown suede vest. Dark brown pants hang where a skirt should be, and I'm unsure about wearing men's pants. Loretta seems to prefer them, and I've even seen Maureen wearing them.

I must know what they feel like and start unbuttoning my dress.

"Whoa, what are you doing?" Garrett calls out, being the gentleman he is, and looks away.

"Oh, please. You've already seen me naked multiple times. And I want to try these pants on."

"Right now?" he asks with a hint of surprise lacing his voice.

"You can leave if you want," I say over my shoulder.

He glances briefly back at me, then moseys over to the writing table. "Can't you wait until I've shown you what I brought you in here for? Then you can try on the pants and whatever else you like?"

"Nope," I say with a playfulness. He may not want to be with me, but ever since the Spirit of the Land awakened a new confidence in me, I'm not afraid of reaching for the things I want. And I kind of want Garrett to want me.

I toss my dress on the floor and stand there in my cotton chemise and long drawers. After pulling off the clothesline pins and setting them on the nearby bookcase, I open the top of the pants and stare into the two leg sleeves, or whatever you call them. I slip one leg in and then the other, and they're tighter than I expected. "How do you close them? I can't walk around like this."

Garrett faces me and laughs. "What are you wearing under the pants?" His laughter vanishes as his gaze moves from the bulge at my waist, up my body to the thin chemise, which barely conceals the dark outlines of the peaks of my breasts. Normally, I'd feel exposed without my long sleeves and high-collar blouse, but not with Garrett. My bare arms and neckline are there for him to touch if he wants—though, I know he doesn't.

I glance at my undergarments and then up to him. "They're drawers. It's a new trend. I overheard some women gossiping about how these are much better than the full-body garments we normally wear. They may have more material, but that's needed to provide more airflow beneath our dresses and skirts."

He tugs at the extra fabric sticking out of the top. "Well, you can't wear those *drawers* if you want to wear pants. There's too much going on and they won't fasten closed," he says, waving a hand at my waist. Then he laughs again, shaking his head while staring at the mess billowing out the top of my pants.

"Well, Persephone must've had something more fitting to wear under these pants. I can't go around wearing nothing!"

Still chuckling, Garrett helps me search the room. He opens the trunk and stands there staring down at what's inside. "I think this might be what you're looking for."

I come over. There're some garments piled to one side and trinkets carefully lined up on the other side. Before I search through the clothes, I remove one of the bottles. There's a clear liquid inside, and its label reads *Vampire Deterrent*. I uncork the top and bring it to my nose. Instantly, I gag and quickly return the cork.

"Damn," Garrett says, waving a hand in front of his face. "I can smell the garlic from here."

Returning the bottle to the trunk, I sweep my gaze over the other labels and decide I'll have to investigate each one more later. Then, I turn my attention to the silky fabric piled on the other side. Lifting one garment, I stand up straight and hold the pair of white satin shorts at eye level.

Garrett is also looking at them. He swallows and then clears his throat. "Yeah, those should do." He then turns around. "Try those."

And I do. I remove the pants and my drawers and slip on the shorts. I'm going to assume they're clean, and it feels a bit off wearing another woman's undergarments, but if I'm going to wear these darn pants, then, well, I'm wearing her shorts.

"Hmm," I say, dragging a hand over the front, sides, and back. I've never felt anything so luxurious before. The fabric is the smoothest material I've ever touched, and there's a satisfying coolness to it too. "I could get used to these," I whisper, which causes Garrett to turn and look.

His eyes go wide, staring at the shorts. "You haven't put the pants on yet?"

He doesn't turn away or repeat instructions to put the pants on. Instead, he stares at my legs while sucking in his bottom lip. "I shouldn't be here while you're doing this," he whispers.

Except he doesn't leave.

He does, however, take a step closer.

"I don't want you to leave," I say. "You still haven't shown me what you brought me in here for."

"I need you to get dressed. Right. Now. I-I don't want either of us to get hurt." His voice is so low, so fragile.

"There's not much up here that's going to hurt us," I say, twisting his words. "You know, just because you don't want to fall in love with anyone, doesn't mean you can't still have intimate relations with them. We could—"

He doesn't let me finish, taking a wide step to close the space between us. He wraps his arms around my waist and pulls me to him. His hands slip up my chemise, caressing my back while his mouth presses against mine. I reach up and run my fingers through his short beard as he parts his lips. Our kiss deepens, and he lifts me up, my back hitting the wall where the clothes hang. I wrap my legs around his waist as one of his hands comes to the front, still under the chemise, and cups my breast.

A low groan rises from his throat as he dips his head, his forehead resting against mine. I kiss the side of his face while his thumb rubs my nipple. A pleasurable ache swells within me, craving more…more kisses, more touching, and more of him wanting me.

I lift my hips and press against him. He breathes heavy, his mouth breaking from mine only long enough to catch his breath as his hand slides down my back, along the satin shorts, until his fingers find skin. He moves up my thigh, slips beneath the soft fabric, and squeezes my bottom cheek.

"Bex." He says my name as if he's parched and begging for water. "If we do this, you need to know it's just to appease the urges we're feeling in the moment. That's it. And I don't think I can—"

I lift his face with my hands and bring my mouth to his, stopping him from finishing that sentence. He presses his body harder against mine. The clothespins holding up the garments hanging on the wall press into my back. I ignore the discomfort and wrap my arms around his shoulders, keeping him close.

When he breaks away, lips gently kissing my cheek, then my jaw, then down my neck, I tell him, "Let's not think about tomorrow." My voice is breathless as I suck in more air as if preparing myself to hold it again. "We're two consenting adults needing one night of pleasure."

He lifts his head and locks eyes with me. "One night," he repeats, as if giving in to his inner conflict.

"One night," I say, soaking in the hunger and desire humming from every part of him.

He hoists my body up, to get a better hold of me, before carrying me out of the private study. Instead of taking me to the four-post bed, he climbs the stairs I'd first noticed in the secret closet that lead up to the loft. It's dark up there, with only a small round window, where moonlight shines down directly over a bed. There's no wooden frame, just a giant mattress on the floor covered in simple white linens.

Slowly he lowers me onto the plush edge of the bed. I scoot back, and lay there, arms spread out to my sides, in nothing but these fancy undershorts and my thin chemise. He unbuttons his shirt and slowly takes it off, never breaking from my eyes.

Then I see it. The same brand Booker has. The same one I now have. It sits on the left side of his chest above his heart. I sit up and get to my knees, reaching up to trace the circle outline and the upside-down A. "Garrett, you're an aber—"

"Yes." He stares down at me, his smooth, bare chest rising with each heavy breath. "We don't know each well enough to trust one another, yet there's something about you, Rebecca Rose Ellington, that constantly intrudes on my thoughts, no matter how I try and distract myself. You're all I think about, and I've tried to convince myself that this," he gestures a pointed finger between us, "can't happen. Love will ruin us from doing our job to protect the town and—"

"And the grandeur junction of lines, yeah, yeah. You're ruining the mood," I say, rubbing my hands up the hard muscles of his abdomen and over his chest.

"Bex," he says my name then groans.

My hands find their way to the top of his pants. "Look, I'm not ready to fall in love with anyone. I know what it's like to lose someone and then grieve. And I'd be lying if I said I didn't think about you a lot."

He lowers himself to the floor, kneeling next to the mattress. Our faces mere inches away, he says, "So we understand one another."

I nod, and lean back, returning to my position lying on the bed.

His gaze travels from my head down to my shorts. Then, he softly confesses, "I don't think I can do one night of pleasure—not with you." He drags his hands over his thighs.

I sit up on my elbows and press one foot to his chest. He lifts my leg and kisses the inside of my calf, then leans forward, kissing higher, until he's reached the inside of my thigh. The short scruff of his beard rubs against my skin, and I can't help the moan that escapes. He's teasing me, and I want to slap him for it. Then, he lifts his head and looks at me. My heart is pounding, as though a wild fever has come over me, and he's the medicine I need to cure this insatiable hunger. I've never wanted anything more than I want this man right now.

He holds my gaze as he slides his hand up my leg and beneath the satin shorts, not stopping until he finds my heat. My back arches, my head falling back as my arms give way and I sink into the thick white quilt. He moves inside me slowly, exploring, pumping two fingers in a steady rhythm. My hands clutch the quilt, fabric clenched tight as he presses deeper into my core.

He slips his fingers out and grabs the top of the shorts, pulling them off before taking me by the hips. With a hard tug, he drags my body closer to him. My head is still spinning from the bliss he ignited seconds ago, and I don't register him lowering himself, replacing his fingers with his mouth. His tongue now having the chance to explore where his fingers have just caressed.

"Garrett!" I scream his name, not caring who hears me. "What are you doing?" I've never heard of a man putting his mouth on this part of a woman's body. What other sensual secrets does this man know?

The world around me blurs, and my arms, legs, and torso all go numb with a rapture like nothing I've ever felt—by my own hands or from my late husband's. The pleasure blooms and I let out a cry as I reach my peak, the explosion of joy dripping out. He gives me one more good suck before turning his head to gently kiss the inside of my thigh. As he straightens up into a more comfortable sitting position, he stares down at me.

What might a night be like if we actually took off *all* our clothes?

He brings up the quilt, folding it over me. "You need to rest. I can show you Persephone's maps tomorrow. Or you can find them yourself, now that you have the key to her private study."

I hug the edge of the quilt against my chest. "Won't you stay a bit longer?"

Shaking his head, he gets to his feet and grabs his shirt. "I almost gave in, Bex. You almost had me."

"I wasn't trying to trap you," I say honestly. "I think there's something between us, and I don't want to lose you."

He buttons up his shirt and smiles. The moonlight barely reaches him as he stands in the doorway to the loft. "You'll never lose me. I'll always be here for you. I'm here for everyone who lives in Gravers Junction."

"Is this how you treat all the residents of Gravers Junction?"

He chuckles. "No, Bex. And I can't believe I wasn't strong enough to keep my distance. I thought I could. You need to understand that my top priority is ensuring the safety of this place. I can't fall in love or be with anyone, not while I have a duty to protect this town and the people who live in it."

My heart fractures at his words. I want to argue and say he can have both, but something in me tells me it may appear needy. No, he needs to figure this out on his own time. I don't want to pressure him into something he isn't fully comfortable with.

"I respect that," I say, which causes his expression to pinch.

"You do? I mean, good." He nods. "Yeah, good. All right, well then, I'll leave you to get some sleep or go and change, whatever… It's your business."

"I think I'm going to take a nice, long, hot bath," I say, throwing the quilt aside and getting to my feet. His gaze dips one last time, taking me in as I slip the undershorts on, slow and deliberate.

He smiles, his eyes lingering, soaking in the tease. He looks like he wants to stay, but then he steps back, as if his mind knows exactly what would happen if he does.

"Goodnight, Bex." He turns and disappears down the stairs.

Challenge accepted, I think to myself. He wants to deny the feelings he's bottling up inside. Well, that is going to come back to bite him in the ass. I'm willing to let him learn this lesson the hard way, because I know deep down inside, Garrett Redthorne is madly in love with me.

TWENTY-ONE

BEX

Over the next two days, I shadow different folks and learn more about their individual jobs and the many ways they lock up before sunset. Garrett has mysteriously disappeared from town. Booker says it's because he asked him to check on his hound dogs, but I know Garrett needed to put some space between him and me.

Booker and Maureen take turns sitting with me, doing what Garrett was supposed to be doing—teaching me about the laws of this land and the supernaturals that live in it. I try not to make it too obvious that I'm annoyed that the sheriff hightailed it out of town.

"You reek of frustration and desire," Booker says, shifting from telling me about the werewolf alpha pack council to addressing my lack of interest. Even though I am interested and listening. I can do both, listen and think about what an ass Garrett's being.

"Desire?" That word's got my attention. "And who might I be desiring?"

Booker laughs, running a hand through his thick black hair, then dragging his hand over his matching beard. "You're too easy to read, my dear. You wear your emotions all over your face. Plus"—he leans in closer—"we werewolves can smell emotions, if they're strong enough. And if we can smell them, then that means the person isn't thinking straight— their emotions are clouding their judgment. And that's the perfect time for a predator to strike."

I pick up on his true meaning. "Right. Clear my head and get focused."

"Always. Bex, you can't ever let your guard down. Not out here in Graveyard Territory."

Turning in my seat on the picnic table out behind the inn, I face the open plains. "Is it all like this?"

Booker, who's sitting on the other side of the picnic table, looks out to the horizon. "Like what?"

"The rest of the territory—is it all flat like this?"

"Most of it, yes. Some areas are rougher, especially along the western and southern regions. The north is colder. Mostly prairie land, with a few rivers. The mountain range to the west belongs to an aberrant race of half-demons known as darkotas."

"Demons? Like actual demons? The ones they say torture evil souls in the afterlife? Those things are real?"

Booker cocks his head and shrugs one shoulder. "I don't know about the afterlife part. But there's a longtime rumor, one that's become widely accepted, that the ley lines caused a tear between two worlds somewhere in Graveyard Territory.

That tear supposedly brought the aberrants into the human world. I don't know how true it is. People just stopped caring where we came from and decided it was explanation enough."

"Humans don't know the shit that lives out here," he adds. "And for some strange reason, all the aberrants prefer it that way."

"Even the demons?" I ask, now turned in my seat and facing Booker.

"Half-demons. I don't know what the other half is, but a whole demon doesn't have a solid body." He points a finger and pokes my arm. "They need a body to have any tangible activity. So, we call the ones who do have bodies half-demons. Or darkotas."

"So, they could still be a whole demon self, just contained." I don't know why I'm trying to make light of the topic. It's scary to think about fighting one of these things, the original-source kind or the half-breed kind.

A howl erupts, and Booker shifts in his seat to look out past the oak tree toward the barn. "Hunter's been doing that a lot lately. He must be missing his new friend—your sister."

"You think that's why he's been howling a lot more this afternoon?"

"Maybe."

I think about Nina, who still has another few days before she returns. Boy, I have a lot to share with her when she gets back. The ley lines, Ruby's garden cage, Ruby being a supernatural, and of course, my night with Garrett.

Damn that man. I should take Tumbleweed and ride out to Booker's place and tell him to his face how ridiculous he's being.

Hunter howls again, and I swear the ground rumbles. I look to Booker and ask, "Is he trying to escape his room?"

Booker stands and sniffs the air. "I don't think that was him." He steps out from the picnic table and moves closer to the plains, where the tall grass starts. After a few quiet moments, he abruptly turns to me and shouts, "Get everyone inside! Go now!"

I jump to my feet. "But it's daylight! They can't attack during the day! You said so yourself—"

"Bex! Stop talking and go tell everyone to get inside!"

Wearing my new pants, my legs able to move more freely, I run alongside the inn to the main road and shout, "Get inside! Everyone, hurry, get inside!"

No one questions my warning. They all drop whatever it is they're holding and head for the closest door. Some even run out of their way to get to a different building. This isn't their first time securing the town on a whim.

I look back at the picnic table. Booker's gone. Gopher's barking by the old oak tree. I can't leave the poor guy out here to face whatever threat is coming. I hurry over to the scruffy dog. "Come on, Gopher. We need to get inside!"

A woman rushes over and scoops up the black dog, even though he's bigger than a sack of potatoes. "Come on," she says, struggling to talk from the strain of carrying Davie's dog. We reach the back door of the inn, but it's locked. I bang on the door and shout, "Hey! Let us in!"

The woman drops Gopher and stares out at the plains stretching out behind town. "Oh, my," she whispers, and I turn around to see what she's gawking at.

A long line of dust wafts in the air, and the ground beneath us trembles. The woman spins on her feet and starts pounding her fists on the door. Gopher stands in a defensive stance, tail straight, and barks at the incoming threat. He then takes off, disappearing into the tall grass.

Stupid dog. I look up at the line of dust getting closer. One time Levi took me to the stockyard, and we watched the men herd a group of cattle from out in the field into a pen. The dust they kicked up filled the air, much like what's heading our way.

It's a stampede of some kind.

"We need to get inside!" The woman whose name I've forgotten turns and runs. "Come on! They're all probably in the parlor or underground!"

I run after her, guilty about leaving Gopher behind.

In the center of town, there are still people racing about. What the hell are they all doing? "Get inside!" I shout. "There's a stampede coming our way!"

Maureen comes out of the inn and hurries over to me. "Are you sure?"

I nod. "Are there wild animals that often go rampant now and then?" Once, my parents told me and Nina about a herd of buffalo off their normal route that trampled over my father's crops.

Maureen shakes her head. "No, not in these parts. The water source is too far underground for them to reach. Those kinds of animals are mostly south or out west."

"Well, they're traveling east today."

"Shit!" Maureen says, cursing at the number of people still outside, trying to secure the town. She hurries out into the middle of the street and hollers, "Don't worry about locking up! It's not a raid or an attack! It's—" Her words are cut off by the ear-piercing shrieks that come from the first creatures that run by both ends of town. Everyone freezes where they stand, watching the giant bugs stampede through the prairie.

"I think we're safe!" I shout over the shrieks and ground pounding.

My words come too soon, and the herd veers, now coming straight into town. And instead of plowing through the buildings, they climb up and over the buildings. They're giant insects, about the size of a large goat, with pale yellow legs that bend like a grasshopper's, with sharp barbs trailing the hind legs. The lower part of their bodies are protected by a hard plating, with light and dark bands of color. And their bulbous heads are smooth with two long antennae sticking out the top front.

"Maureen!" I shout, and release the sandropes from my arms. I whip my right arm out, snapping the tip at a creature about to collide into the older woman. It hisses, then screeches, as if realizing its stumbled upon something to eat. It looks at me and skitters closer. Maureen stays still while it moves past her, then when there's a clear path, she hurries to the platform sidewalk. Another one hops off the side of the building right on top of Maureen. She falls against the wood planks, rolling over and screaming.

I reel in one of my sandropes and hold out my hand, commanding a dust storm to blind the creature rushing at me. It works, and I race around the blustering dust cloud to get to Maureen. A shriek catches my attention, and I look up just as another one skitters over the roof and down the side of the building. More and more keep coming. We need to get inside.

"Hey, you disgusting critters!" Booker shouts from across the way. He's standing in the open barn door.

What is he doing? If they get inside the barn and attack the animals—but then an enormous wolf sprints out from inside the barn. Hunter lunges for the closest bug and rips it in half with one snap of his teeth. The insects are comparable to his overwhelming size. He doesn't hesitate to move to the next one and rip its head right off its body. A nearby critter sits back on its barbed hind legs and lifts its bulbous head to the sky and shrieks three abrupt calls. This has the rest of them stopping where they are—whether they were attacking a person or running through town—and then pivoting their direction to the south, leaving town.

Once the dust settles, Booker and I hurry over to Maureen. She's bleeding pretty badly in her shoulder and side. "Dammit," she curses. "That nasty bug took a good chunk out of my stomach." She winces as she presses a hand to the bloodstained spot along her stomach.

Booker helps her to her feet, and with one arm over his shoulders, he helps her into the inn. Ruby, Sheamus, and the woman who tried to save Gopher all run out, right past me and to those who were also attacked.

Damn Garrett for not being here. I know it's not his fault these bug things attacked or stormed the town, but he should've been here to help the townsfolk. I'm getting a bit tired of all these unexpected surprises, like how evil can strike even when the sun's still up. Oh, that man is going to get an earful when I see him again.

TWENTY-TWO

BEX

It's been three days since the attack, making it day six since Nina first left Gravers Junction. She'll hopefully be back today. With Maureen barely conscious as she recovers from the surgery her medics had to perform, and Garrett still absent, Ruby and Booker have taken to running things in town. There's a medic corridor farther down the underground tunnel at the opposite end of where the inn is, and that's where we've moved all the injured folks. It's a large room with eight beds, every one of them filled with an injured person. Some more dire than others, but Booker wanted them all in one place rather than the medics doing house calls to each of their homes.

Maureen is the only one isolated in her room. Her home, also underground, is just below the inn. There's a large living room with a wood stove. There are other rooms attached to the living space, but I don't snoop to see what's behind the doors. Rather, I stick to the closest door after walking into her place. She lies in her bed, a beautiful patchwork quilt spread out over her as she sleeps. I refresh her pitcher of water before pouring the blood-soaked water from the basin into my pitcher.

"Bex," Maureen whispers to me, stirring.

"You're awake!" I say, excited she's pulling through the worst of it. Setting the pitcher down, careful not to spill the bloody water, I sit on the edge of the bed to hold her hand. "I'm here."

With dreadful anticipation, her eyes gloss over, tears ready to spill. "Did we lose anyone?"

I take a deep breath before answering her, not wanting to be the person who has to tell her. I nod. "Three people."

Her chin trembles, and she brings a hand to her mouth. The scratches along her hand and arm are healing, unlike those poor souls we lost a few days ago. Their wounds took them to their graves.

"How do we get word to Garrett?" I hope she understands I'm not asking for me.

She shakes her head. "We don't."

Booker steps into the room, then moves to the footboard. "Good, you're awake. Come first light, I'll head out and find him. If he's where I think he is, we should be back before dark."

Maureen looks down at her quilt, her fingers tapping the fabric. "What day is it? How many more days do we have?"

Booker sighs and says, "Cletus will return tomorrow, ma'am."

She shakes her head. "Then, no. We need you here. Garrett knows what tomorrow is. He'll be back in time."

"Are you sure?" I ask, knowing she's right, but the reassurance would be nice to hear.

"I'm sure," she says, and the confidence in her tone makes me feel better already.

"Ruby will bring you some soup shortly." Booker turns to the door. "Come on, Bex. Let's let Maureen get some rest."

A man comes running into Maureen's living room, shouting, "The stagecoach has returned!"

I move to the doorway, almost knocking over the pitcher. I carefully settle it before rushing out of Maureen's home. My feet aren't moving fast enough. All I want is to see Nina. Thank the stars, my sister has returned in one piece!

Both Booker and I rush outside. The sun hasn't set yet, so they made it in plenty of time. Nina hops out of the carriage and rushes at me. We embrace so tightly I swear we almost topple to the ground.

"Dammit, where have you been?" I ask, not caring that part of her pale blonde braid got stuck in the corner of my mouth.

"Language," she says with a chuckle. "I leave you alone for a week and you're cursing like a rancher. Next thing you know you'll be spitting on the ground and gambling at the saloon!"

We share a good laugh before we break apart. She gives my hand a tight squeeze and says, "Oh, I have so much to tell you. And not all of it is good."

I widen my eyes and nod. "Same. We were attacked—well, not really attacked, more like an unexpected stampede of wild insects the size of Hunter came through town, killing a few folks."

"What?!" Nina says with a gasp. "Insects? Is Hunter okay?"

"Yes, he's fine. So are Booker, Ruby, and Sheamus."

"What about Maureen? And Garrett?"

"Maureen got hurt pretty badly, but she'll live. The sheriff wasn't here when it happened."

She rubs a hand on my face and smiles. It's as if she can already tell there's something wrong between me and Garrett. "Come on, let's help carry this stuff inside, and then we can talk more."

After helping everyone unload the carriage, with a lot of familiar things Nina packed up and brought from our farm, we head inside the inn to have some supper. Ruby set out a large ceramic soup bowl for everyone to serve themselves. I know she's still down in the infirmary, helping tend to the injured. The ceramic soup bowl is another gorgeous item they have here with a fitted lid that has a small cutout for the ladle. I take one bowl before lifting the lid and ladling out some vegetable soup.

"Where's everyone?" Nina asks.

"Probably down visiting Maureen. She's not able to get up yet after her surgery."

"Surgery?" Nina asks with a surprised tone. "Do they have a hospital here?"

I shake my head and sit in my usual seat at the side of the table. "No, but they have an impressive infirmary with a large stock of medical supplies."

Nina sits next to me. "Where do you think they get all that stuff from?"

I blow on a spoonful, the wafting steam vanishing. "They must make supply runs east, I assume. Now, tell me about what happened. What's this good and bad news?"

Nina waves a hand in front of her mouth, obviously not waiting for her soup to cool. "Oh, well," she tries to start, but she's still recovering from her hot soup. "Ambrose Redding required my coming to town and signing some papers. I tried to tell him I wasn't the owner of the property or the land, but he insisted I come into town. So I had to ride into town for that."

"How annoyed were your traveling companions for having to stay the night on the farm?" I ask, thinking they'd want to get home as fast as possible.

A smile spreads, and she holds off taking another bite to explain, "Oh, they loved it out there. I swear, they all slept most of the morning, just so they could stay up late outside by the campfire. They were staring at the stars, drinking and eating by the fire, having a grand old time."

"I guess they don't get to go outside at night too often, huh?"

"No, they don't." Nina giggles. Then in a more serious tone, she says, "I don't like that Ambrose Redding guy."

"No one does," I quickly agree. "But he's got money, and we couldn't get a loan from the bank, so he was the best option."

"Levi should've talked to our father first before dealing with that slimy man. I reckon, he's shadier than the evil things lurking out here in Graveyard Territory."

I wave my spoon at her before taking another bite. "So, what did he want?"

"Are you wearing pants, Rebecca Rose Ellington?" Nina reaches under the table and pinches my leg.

"Ow! Yes! Don't pinch me!" I laugh while swiping her hand away. "They're actually quite comfortable, and much easier to fight in when I need to. Now, finish telling me about Redding."

"Did someone say Redding, as in Ambrose Redding?" Booker asks, walking into the dining room. He grabs a bowl and serves himself some soup.

I recall the other day how Booker had asked me if I knew Mr. Redding. I turn in my seat and as Booker sits across from us, I ask, "How exactly do you know him?"

He snorts a chuckle. "Everyone knows that weasel. He's no good, and you should stay clear of him and his dealings." Without waiting for the soup to cool, he shovels a heaping spoonful into his mouth.

"Why's that?" Nina asks before I can.

Booker swallows the hot soup and tells us, "That man is always out for blood and power. Remember, I told you how some men are worse than the aberrants out here?" I nod, and he continues, "Well, he's bloody one of them. He's in cahoots with Santana."

"The vampire?" I ask.

He nods, looking impressed at my ability to retain some of the stuff I learned these past few days. "Santana isn't just any vampire. He's what you call a *souleech*, an aberrant that feeds on emotional energy."

"Wait," Nina cuts in, and asks, "Didn't Cletus say that witch of his also feed on a person's essence?"

"Viola, and yes. She's also a souleech, but not a vampire. The ability to drain a person's life force is a rare trait that's only possible in aberrants that are born aberrants and not changed. So, if you get bit by a werewolf, you become a werewolf, but you'll never be a souleech. Witches, vampires, darkotas, entomonians, stonians, and any other aberrant born into this world have the chance of being born with a second power."

Nina sets her spoon down. "There's so much to learn about this secret world you all live in."

"You too, darlin'. You're even more rare than those with the souleech power. I don't know much about your kind, but I do know that a winds whisperer is said to be quite powerful."

"I don't know about that. I don't feel powerful." Nina leans back in her chair.

"Anyway, I would avoid crossing paths with Santana, but at the same time if you're ever looking for a drifter to hire, a night of pleasure, or a place to gamble your soul away—then head to the Sundown Saloon."

"Do you think that's where Garrett is?" my mouth asks before my brain can stop the words from slipping free. "Sorry, it's none of my business where he spends his time."

Booker winks at me, and heat flushes my face. "No, ma'am. That's not his scene. Like I said before, he's probably holed up at my place with Ranger and Otis."

"Your hound dogs?" I guess.

He nods. "They know and trust Garrett. Whatever squabble you two got into a few nights ago must've hit him hard. He's come out to stay with me before, but I can't recall a time when he's been away from Gravers Junction for this long."

"You think he's hurt, or in danger?" Nina asks.

Booker takes another mouthful and shrugs. "It's a game of survival out there. You ought to be ready for anything if you're out there alone."

"Well, good thing he has Otis and Ranger," I say, trying to reassure myself he's fine.

Knock, knock, knock, knock.

Booker narrows his eyes at the dining room doorway. Slowly, all three of us get up and make our way out into the parlor. From the windows, I can see the sun hasn't set yet. So who's knocking on the front door of the inn? He looks to us and nods, silently telling us to be ready for anything, before opening the door.

Standing out on the front porch is Viola.

"Can we help you, witch?" Booker asks with a snarl.

She looks past the alpha werewolf and me, the new dustslinger, and says to my sister, "We need to talk."

TWENTY-THREE

BEX

Booker stands by the bar while Nina and I sit at a table with Viola. All three of us know Booker can hear well enough, even if we lower our voices to a whisper. He's a werewolf, and he has exceptional hearing.

"I don't know you, so what makes you think I'm going to help you?" Nina asks, narrowing her icy blue eyes at the witch.

Before she can answer, I ask, "Does Cletus know you're here?"

That must have a straightforward answer, because she doesn't hesitate to shake her head. There doesn't seem to be any concern about him not knowing either. "He doesn't believe me when I tell him about the threat to the land. It's coming sooner than I thought."

"Let's circle back to why you're here. What do you need from me?" Nina asks again.

Viola sits back in her chair. She's wearing a dark purple blouse that cinches around the neckline, that's also been pulled low over her shoulders. It's the first time I've ever seen a woman wear a corset on the outside, and one that's not white. Hers is black. She wears black pants, but they're loose around her thighs and fitted from her knees down, tucked into her tall black riding boots. She wears a gun belt around her waist, with one pistol secured in its holster.

"I've come to make a deal with you." She's not here to make a deal with the dustslinger. She's staring right at my sister.

"I'm listening," Nina responds in a low, serious tone.

"This isn't happening. No way, no how." I stand up, and Viola raises her hand, palm out facing me. My feet lift off the ground and before I can summon my dust power, I'm suspended in the air in one of the witch's soapy bubbles again.

"Viola," Booker growls from the bar.

"What? I'm not hurting her. I just need her to be quiet while the mystics talk."

Mystics? What is she blabbering on about? My sister doesn't break eye contact with the witch.

"I know where you come from," Viola says, her hand still above her head, holding me suspended in the air. With her other hand she leans forward, reaching across the table, and drags a hand down one of Nina's braids. "You're one of those Glacic northerners."

"Let me down! I promise to let you talk this out, whatever it is!"

Viola closes her fist, and the soapy bubble vanishes. I land on the ground, my balance thrown off. Nina doesn't even look my way or offer to help me up after I fall on my ass.

"If you know where I come from, and you know what I can do, then you know I'm more powerful than you." Nina rests her chin on her hand that's propped up on the table. The front door bursts open, slamming against the wall as a rush of storm wind fills the parlor. With a wicked smile, Nina has summoned the winds.

I stand and stretch my hands out at arm's length, and using my own magic, I force the dust that's come inside away from the table. The wind grows more violent, circling the room like a cyclone. It's murky and dark, carrying a lot of dirt from the road. I can't even see Booker at the bar anymore.

"Enough!" Viola abruptly stands and shouts. "There's no need to demonstrate. I believe you, which is why I convinced Cletus to give you a week before coming back to take you and that rogue mutt away."

Nina closes her eyes, and the wind circling the room floods back outside, closing the front door behind it. I've never seen her do anything like that. She leans back in her chair. "Speak your piece. And if you call Hunter a *mutt* again, I'll steal the air from your lungs and watch you suffocate."

Caught off guard, I gasp. "What the hell, Nina?" She's never behaved in such a manner before.

Booker's catching his breath behind the bar. He holds up a hand and shouts, "I'm good—I'm all right. Don't worry about me."

Viola lowers herself into her chair again. "If I can guarantee Cletus won't take you or *Hunter*"—she says his name as if she's tasted something rotten—"when he comes tomorrow, I want something in return. A simple favor."

"What kind of favor?" Nina asks.

"That's to be determined at another time. For now, I'm your best option against what's coming for you and your *friend*."

Nina smiles. "I don't need your help. I can handle Cletus by myself," she says with a hint of pride in her voice.

"You attack Cletus in a transaction that he has every right to see carried out, then you'll bring down the wrath of the alpha council. And not just to you and your sister, but to Gravers Junction and its people." Viola's gaze intensifies. "I'm trying to prevent more bloodshed." She leans her elbows on the table and stares at Nina. "Take my offer."

I jump in with a question. "What will Cletus want in place of Hunter and Nina? He's not going to leave here empty-handed, will he?"

Viola sighs while rubbing the tips of her long black nails with her thumb. "He will."

"So, like I said. We don't need to make a deal with you because I can handle him," Nina reiterates.

I lean over and whisper to Nina, "She's not wrong. From what Booker's told me about the alpha council, they live by a strong code. My interference caused this whole mess, so it has to be me who fixes it."

"And how do you plan on doing that?" Nina asks, anger lacing her tone.

"I can challenge him to a fight."

"No!" Booker says at the same time Viola laughs.

He comes out from behind the bar and sits at the table with us. "We'll think of something." He then looks at Nina. "It's a good deal. Take the deal."

"But we don't know what this favor is she'll ask of Nina?" I point out.

"Deal," Nina says before anyone addresses my concerns.

Viola jumps to her feet, and her boots pound the wooden floorboards as she makes her way to the door. "Oh, and I forgot to mention, he's coming tonight."

"What?" I ask. "We have until tomorrow."

Booker curses under his breath, then mutters, "He's coming at midnight, isn't he?"

The witch smiles before walking out of the inn.

TWENTY-FOUR

BEX

I never thought the day would come where the words *we have to trust the witch* would leave my mouth. Viola told us she can convince Cletus not to take my sister or Hunter. And we'll have to trust that she'll make good on her promise.

"We need an alternative offer, just in case things go south," Nina reminds those of us in the room, which is me, Booker, Murphy, Sheamus, Loretta, and Ruby. Everyone except Booker has been quiet since arriving, as if they aren't normally privy to decision-making meetings.

The grandfather clock on the other side of the parlor from the piano chimes eleven times, signaling we've got one hour left before midnight.

Loretta nudges Murphy in the arm and says, "We can round up the deputies and position them around town. No weremutt…no offense to present company—"

"Some taken," Booker replies.

Loretta finishes, "…will be able to see them."

"But they'll be able to sniff them out, but you do whatever you think will keep the town safe," Booker states, seemingly annoyed with the redheaded gunslinger.

"I can get Trigger to cover the roof of the inn," Murphy suggests.

"Yeah, put him up there in the cage with a watcher. Good idea," Booker says, nodding to Murphy.

I'm not sure who this guy is or what a watcher is, so I ask. "Who is Trigger and why are you putting him in a cage on the inn's roof with a watcher?"

"A watcher," Loretta answers, "is someone who watches the surrounding area. So no one sneaks up on you from behind."

"And Trigger—his birth name is actually Trent—is our town sharpshooter. He's also one of Gravers Junction's deputies."

Ruby leans over from her chair next to me and says, "And there's a cage up there that's like my garden cage. As an extra layer of security."

I pocket the name and his title for later when I meet him. For now, I'm grateful to know there's someone who can potentially take out Cletus if needed. I look around the room. "And who will be his watcher?"

Murphy whistles, and Davie and Gopher come strolling into the parlor. I'm happy to see the scrappy dog didn't get killed by the giant bugs. "Davie can do it," Murphy offers. To his son, he says, "Go get your rifle, and lock up that damn dog."

Davie nods, then disappears into the back hall.

"What about Hunter?" Loretta asks. "Do we bring him out or keep him locked up?"

I can't read Booker's expression, and then I realize why. He knows it's not his decision to make. Even though he offered himself up to be Hunter's alpha, if Hunter ever accepted, they'd both be on the kill list with the alpha council. What exactly that means, I have no idea.

But then I see the hurt in Booker's expression as he looks to Nina.

"Oh, no. Please tell me Hunter didn't already pledge his loyalty to you?" I ask, facing my sister. "You're not a werewolf!" He stood by her side that night, protecting her. The rogue wolf's loyalty is to my sister.

"And he can do whatever the hell he wants!" Hearing my sister curse feels wrong. For me, it was invigorating, like a rebellious act. But coming out of Nina's mouth, it feels like anger has gotten the best of her sweet nature.

Nina stands and says, "I'll get him. He needs to be there. We can't trust Viola to keep her word. And we don't want Cletus to think we're trying to deceive him by hiding Hunter or me. We need to be out there when he arrives." She walks toward the back hall, knowing to use the tunnels rather than go outside. Holding on to the door frame, she tells everyone, "If she keeps her word, and Cletus is open to an alternative, you guys are going to have to think up a deal that'll appease him." And with that, she leaves the parlor.

"I don't know much about your cousin," I say, looking to Booker. "What's something he'd want?"

"Where to begin?" he says with a snort.

Everyone throws out ideas from firearms to livestock, and even baked goods, which of course was Ruby's suggestion. Time passes, and we're less than ten minutes from midnight. Murphy already sent Davie to get Trent and head up to the cage on the roof of the inn. We're all sitting around, staring at the clock, still unsure about what we're going to offer Cletus in exchange for Hunter and Nina, when Garrett walks in from the front door.

"I got it!" He holds up a small wooden box and looks over the entire group before locking eyes with Booker.

"Geez, man. Nothing like getting' back at the eleventh hour!" Booker stands from his seat and weaves through the tables until he's right in front of Garrett. He takes the small box and looks inside. He closes it, not sharing the contents with the rest of us.

"Can I show this to Maureen?" Booker asks.

Garrett nods, and Booker waves for Murphy to follow. Sheamus makes his way to his piano. I don't know what the meaning is behind the song he starts playing, but I don't care. All I care about is that Garrett is here.

I walk over to him, and he removes his sunrider hat and holds it against his chest. "Sorry I didn't tell you I was leaving."

"It's fine," I say with all the calm and collected nerves I can muster. "I'm just happy you're not hurt."

Loretta marches over and punches Garrett in the arm. "Damn, boss! Glad to see you're not dead!"

He smiles at his deputy. "Get into position across the way. Wait for my signal if we need you. Tell the other deputies to get into position and buckle down. And send Trigger up on the roof."

"Already on it, boss!" She adjusts her two pistols at her waist and then hurries out the back of the parlor.

Ruby stands from her seat at the table and says, "I'm going to lock myself in Maureen's place and make sure she stays safe. If those bastards get inside, I'll protect her with my life."

"Thank you, Ruby."

It's just him and me and, well, Sheamus, but he's preoccupied with his music. I stare into Garrett's eyes. "Where did you go?"

"An idea popped into my head about what we can offer Cletus to either forfeit his retribution or at least give us more time to find something he might want more than your sister and Hunter."

I glance back at the doorway where Booker took the small box to show Maureen. "What's in the box?"

"A family heirloom of some sort."

"Something that belongs to your family?"

"My family is a complicated mess. One that we can get into tomorrow if we survive the night." He steps closer, tucking a strand of my hair behind one of my ears. "I really am sorry I left without telling you where I was going."

"Have you changed your mind about…" I lift my chin and look up, as if gesturing to the bedrooms upstairs.

He laughs. "If you're wondering if I've changed my mind about us, then no. I haven't. And you shouldn't be trying to get me to change my mind. We need to stay focused on protecting this town." Silence lingers between us, and after a few heartbeats, he asks, "Can you do that for me?"

No. Dammit. But, at the same time, I understand what he's saying. "I can respect that."

The grandfather clock strikes twelve, and everyone looks to the door when it swings open. "They're here," Nina says, a giant wolf standing by her side.

Murphy and Booker follow Nina and Hunter outside. Garrett grabs my arm the second I go to follow and spins me to face him. "Don't be a hero out there. We've got a plan—a good deal that Cletus will take."

"I can't make any promises. I'll do whatever it takes to protect those I care for, and I've come to care for quite a few things in this town. Ruby's frozen cream being one of them."

He laughs, and it looks good on him. "Always the cheeky one, aren't you?" Then to my sister he asks, "You ready?"

"Let's go make a deal," she says, turning away and walking outside with Hunter on her heels.

TWENTY-FIVE

BEX

Cletus has already dismounted from his beast of a horse and is standing in the middle of town. Viola and another rider linger behind on their horses. The witch doesn't pay any attention to anyone but my sister, and that concerns me. If we survive this, what favor is she going to call in for my sister to do? I don't like it. What I do like is the massive wolf by Nina's side, protecting her. I don't understand it, but I approve of his choice.

"My faithful witch tells me you have an offer for me to consider. Let's hear what you've got!" Cletus shouts from the middle of the street. He tips his black sunrider hat up, just enough so we can see his face. He's wearing similar clothes to when we saw him last, except tonight he's got a strip of black fur hanging from his waistband.

Garrett steps off the porch platform. "I was the one who shot your pup," he confesses. "It wasn't the dustslinger. It was me."

A wide, toothy smile spreads across Cletus's face. "Does Maureen know about this?" Then he looks around, brows pinching, and he asks, "Where she at?"

"She had to travel and was scheduled to return tomorrow. We weren't expecting a midnight visit," Garrett explains. "Now, do you want to hear what I have to offer as an apology?"

Cletus's smile returns. "Sure, why not."

Garrett looks at Booker and gives him a nod. Booker walks out and meets his cousin out in the street. He hands him the wooden box and slowly backs away, not turning his back to our enemy.

"This is a wee-tiny box. I don't know if what's inside will be as good as a rogue werewolf, the sheriff of Gravers Junction, and a mystic of the winds." He laughs and then opens the lid. His amusement immediately falls, and he takes out the gold ring before turning it over at eye level. Then he looks at Garrett. "Where did you get this?"

"Let's say I found it and just kept it for a rainy day."

I recall Garrett telling me it was a family heirloom.

Cletus drops the ring back into the wooden box and slams the lid shut. "Why would you give this to me? Are you trying to start a war between us and those bloodsuckers?"

"No. I thought you could return it, since the owner lost it after being banished from his coven. Your bringing it back rather than keeping it actually puts you in favor with their elder council."

"Lies!" Cletus spits on the dirt before throwing the box onto the ground. "I decline your offer and will keep the original bounty of the woman and the wolf. Now, hand them over!"

My gaze shifts from the angry alpha werewolf to Viola, who now has a fearsome expression on her face, and she's staring across the way at Nina and Hunter.

Cletus marches over to my sister, and I react, pulling myself inward until I disappear from Booker's side to over in the path of Cletus.

He bellows out a laugh. "Oh, it's you again, baby dustslinger! Get out of my way!" He whips out a fist and backhands the side of my face.

Nina screams, "Bex!"

My dustslinger magic reacts, and when his fist contacts my face, he's met with a dust cloud where my cheek should've been. His hand passes through, and the second he's clear, my face returns to its normal self. Not waiting for him to balance himself out, I throw out my sandropes and flick my wrists so the ropes wrap around his entire body.

"You are dead," he says, seething and spitting at me. "Dead! Do you hear me?"

Garrett and Booker creep closer, while Nina and Hunter also stalk closer from behind.

From behind Cletus, the Spirit of the Land appears, floating high in the air. No one else seems to notice her. *"Use the elements, child of dust. Ignite your anger."* Then she fades from view.

Use the elements? Then something sparks inside my mind. And a wicked idea forms. Cletus is struggling to escape my sandropes, and his pups are closing in, ready to strike if Cletus gives the command.

I think about what I want to happen—fire. And then flames ignite, traveling from my hands and down along the sandropes, which are still wrapped around Cletus. "You think you're so clever, don't you, dustslinger?"

"I think so, for a newbie." The flames glow brightly, illuminating the center of town.

"Bex! What are you doing?" Garrett shouts.

"You know," Cletus says, a low growl in his voice, "one word from me and my pups will shred everyone in this town." His arms are bound, and the flames have reached his body. "Will I be your first?" he asks, while staring at me, a test to see if I'm ready to take a life.

And I'm not.

I withdraw the flames and let the sandropes dissipate, sprinkling to the ground.

Nina hurries to my side. "If you touch her, I won't hesitate to kill you." Hunter approaches, standing next to Nina, baring his teeth. From the building next to the barn, Loretta steps outside, her lucky pistols drawn.

Cletus returns to his horse, and before he mounts it, he tells Garrett, "Keep your ring, and your mystic, and the rogue werewolf. I can't promise the council won't put out a bounty for him when I report his whereabouts."

"We'll deal with that when the time comes," Booker shouts to his cousin.

"You still owe me blood," Cletus says after mounting his horse. "I won't forget that." He whistles and waves a finger in the air. Cletus and the other rider leave town, while the werewolves run with a speed so fast, I wouldn't have believed it if I hadn't seen it. The only one left is Viola. She looks to my sister and nods. Nina reciprocates. Then Viola pulls on her horse's reins and she rides out of town.

Thinking about how fast the werewolves just sprinted out of here in their human form, I ask Booker, "Can you run that fast?"

He chuckles. "I'm an old man now. But back in the day, shit, no one could catch me."

"Hunter and I are going to pick out a room inside the inn for us." She's speaking to Garrett. "I'll not have him sleeping in that dark hole you've got him locked up in anymore." Without another word, she walks off, a rogue werewolf by her side.

Loretta and the others all make their way into the inn too. It's late, and I reckon none of them want to stay out here any longer than they have to. I recall Maureen's warning that even though one evil has left, there may be others lurking about. Garrett and I are the last ones standing outside, and we take our time following everyone into the inn.

"I told you not to be a hero," he says.

"I know, but I couldn't let him take my sister."

"That was a neat trick, lighting your sandropes on fire."

"Yeah. It was. I still have a lot to learn about this land."

He holds the door open for me and says, "Today was a win, Bex. But the next confrontation might not go in our favor. You need to practice more with your powers and learn everything there is to know about aberrants in the Graveyard Territory. That's if you decide you're going to stay."

Inside, he locks the door behind us. Sheamus continues playing the piano while we stand there staring at one another.

"I thought you left because of me," I confess.

He smiles. "The world doesn't revolve around you, Bex."

"I know." Then, curious about the ring, I ask, "Did you really think he'd take the ring?"

Garrett removes his sunrider hat off and hangs it on a nearby coat stand. "I did, actually. But I also didn't think he'd think I was setting him up for a conflict with the vampires."

"Who's ring was it?"

"It belongs to my brother's father." He holds the box out and opens the lid. There's the gold ring Cletus held up earlier. In the center of the ring is an embossed rose with thorns on its stem. The rose is black, while the stem and thorns are red. I put two and two together and silently think, *Redthorne. Garrett fucking Redthorne.*

He searches my face and then asks, "Did you make your decision?"

I smile, knowing Nina will support me in this decision, even though we haven't talked about it. "If Gravers Junction will have me, I'd love to be your dustslinger."

A NOTE FROM THE AUTHOR

Thank you for taking the time to read
Secrets of Gravers Junction,
book one in *The Chronicles of a Dustslinger*
a romantic fantasy set in an alternative old west.

More adventures to come in book two!

If you enjoyed this story, please consider leaving a review
and recommending this series to a friend.

For more information about the author, visit:
https://kimberlygrymes.com/

For a deeper experience into this series, visit:
https://www.patreon.com/ChroniclesOfADustslinger

There's no cost to follow for general announcements and
reveals, and you can choose to upgrade later for access to
more detailed content and early chapter releases.

ACKNOWLEDGMENTS

I wasn't kidding about this book and series concept being completely spontaneous after being accepted into the Forbidden Love Book Festival. For other details that can't be revealed, I'd reached out to Bri, the event organizer, with a question. That conversation led to me filling out an author interest form and being accepted to the 2026 Forbidden Love Book Festival.

Then I realized I wouldn't have anything "new" on my table for the event. Well, my ADHD brain wasn't going to accept that. Because I'd created a new pen name, Kay Grymes, for my adult fiction stories, I decided I would write a new book and build up my Kay Grymes author resume. I started writing *Secrets of Gravers Junction* right after Thanksgiving 2025 and finished it on January 2, 2026. My daily word counts were insane, especially for such a busy holiday month!!

Anyhoo. A ginormous thank you to Brianna for sparking my creativity into high gear. I love my other story worlds… but there's something special about writing for adult readers and weaving in some heated romance that brings me such amazing joy. I cannot wait to write more in this story world!!

And the joy really took root after reading feedback from my three beta readers! Hearing their praise really boosted my confidence and my hope that other readers will enjoy it too. So, thank you to my beta readers: author Hope E. Davis, Abbey, and Melissa from @melissathatswhatsheread.

I would also like to give thanks to my copy and line editor, Nikki Mentges with NAM Editorial. As always, she went above and beyond with her edits and feedback. It's always a pleasure to work with Nikki.

The final round of edits, the proofreading stage, I have to admit I was sooo excited for because Aime Sund from Red Leaf Word Services is not only an amazing editor but also a good friend. And I was so excited for her to read this new story with such a specific niche in the fantasy genre. Her feedback and praise raised my excitement even more! Thank you, Aime, for taking the time to support a friend and proofread her story!

I know you've only seen the character artwork on the cover for book one, but I cannot wait to share the character artwork on the other covers in season one of this series. It's been a wonderful experience working with Natascia Mora (Instagram @moranatascia) bringing these characters to life for the cover art.

And I guess I should throw my family into the mix too, lol. They're my biggest supporters and fans. Our middle kiddo even drew Tumbleweed and Frostbite for me! I wouldn't be able to do this author gig without the love and support of my husband, Jim, and our three kiddos, Kayla, Abby, and Chloe. I love and appreciate them all soooo much. We have so much love in our house, which is why it's so easy for me to write tropes like found family, strong compassionate characters, and fun banter.

And to the readers. As much as I write for me, I also write for you. I love that feeling a person gets when they watch a good movie, and since I can't make movies, I'll bring you stories you can escape into. Thank you and keep reading whatever brings you joy!

About the Author

Kimberly/Kay Grymes writes fantasy and romance stories. Kimberly Grymes focuses on YA fantasy while Kay Grymes explores more adult fantasy and romance stories. Her favorite stories to write are found family, and now under her new pen name she can add a splash of heated romance to the mix!

When she's not busy with her author gig, Kimberly enjoys spending time with her family, watching movies and TV shows, reading fantasy books, and playing cozy video games. She and her family reside on the outskirts of Wichita, Kansas, accompanied by their two lively miniature pinschers, Cori and Jubilee.